Love & Laughter Quiz

You know you've got a Matchmaking Mother when:

a) You go shopping with her and all she wants to do is browse the bridal boutique.

b) Her best friend's nephew with the pocket guard and Coke-bottle glasses and the "good job in accounting" always drops by when you're visiting her.

c) She tells you that after your twenty-fifth birthday you might as well join a convent.

If you answered:

a) Give yourself one point

b) Give yourself two points

c) Give yourself three points

The higher the score, the less subtle your matchmaking mother.... Beware the Matchmaking Mother From Hell!

You know you've got a Matchmaking Mother *from Hell* when:

a) She blackmails you into attending your own twenty-fifth birthday party, where you know she's going to spring hopeful fiancés on you.

b) She holds you hostage on her private island that's deserted except for you, and her, and a few suitors *she* has decided should vie for your fair hand.

c) You just can't win. She unknowingly sets you up with the perfect man, and then freaks out when you fall in love.

If you answered:

a) Give yourself four points

b) Give yourself four points

c) Give yourself four points

If you scored any points at all, you've got a Matchmaking Mother from Hell on your hands.

Dear Reader,

Mother knows best—maybe! That's the theme of
our miniseries Matchmaking Mothers (from Hell).
Ruth Jean Dale launches this fun series with
A Royal Pain.

I think we can all relate to meddling mothers, only
these matchmaking moms take events to the extreme.
How is a respectable woman to become a grandmother
unless her offspring cooperates? There's nothing to be
done except to get the kids down the aisle, even if
they go kicking and screaming all the way! Plans are
made, schemes hatched, plots unraveled.

Next month the miniseries continues with Vicki Lewis
Thompson's *One Mom Too Many.* Watch for more
Matchmaking Mothers (from Hell) in the months ahead!

Not to be outdone in amusement is Suzannah Davis's
Heatcrazed! An entire town goes a little crazy during
a heat wave, and the "invasion" of laughter begins.
Suzannah is a longtime popular author familiar to
romance readers. She's also a great fan of "Star Trek"
and "The X-Files," as I think you'll be able to tell from
her delightfully comic take on Fox Mulder's favorite
obsession. Enjoy!

With love and laughter,

Malle Vallik

Malle Vallik
Associate Senior Editor

A ROYAL PAIN
Ruth Jean Dale

Harlequin Books

TORONTO • NEW YORK • LONDON
AMSTERDAM • PARIS • SYDNEY • HAMBURG
STOCKHOLM • ATHENS • TOKYO • MILAN
MADRID • WARSAW • BUDAPEST • AUCKLAND

Many thanks to my daughter, Valerie Duran, who read; my friend Margaret Brownley, who understood; and the nice folks on the net who shared their love of Kansas City barbecue.

ISBN 0-373-44015-4

A ROYAL PAIN

My take on matchmaking mothers from hell is absolute pure fiction. My own sweet little mother not only didn't matchmake, she didn't even seem to understand the basic chemistry that drew two people together— although with four children before she was twenty-one, she should have. When I called to tell her I was engaged, her response stopped me cold. After a long pause, she asked in an extremely puzzled tone, *"Why?"* I thought my reasons should be obvious, but I said, rather indignantly, "Because I love him!" I can only hope our many years of married bliss have proven my truthfulness—and that *A Royal Pain* will attest to my imagination. Because, believe me, this story did *not* come from real life.

—Ruth Jean Dale

Prologue

"TAKE A MEMO, Malcolm."

Lucretia Addison paused in her purposeful pacing to issue the order to her executive assistant. Waiting for him to locate his leather-bound notepad, she lingered before the glass wall of her luxurious suite of offices high atop the Addison Building in the heart of Los Angeles and studied her right-hand man.

Lurking behind that conservative business suit and those rimless eyeglasses was an attractive young man with a mind like a steel trap. Dark-blond hair, thick and shiny, fell loosely into shining waves from a side part. His eyes were blue, his teeth white and gleaming when he smiled.

But so far as Lucretia Addison was concerned, the best thing about him was his unquestioned loyalty—that and his ability to handle the trickiest negotiations and the most sensitive issues. Charles Lawrence, twenty-nine and a native of Kansas City, Missouri, had served for almost two years as the latest incarnation of Lucretia's first Malcolm, one Malcolm Slusher—a long run in the employment of such a demanding boss.

That first Malcolm was long gone, but ever after, Lucretia had called all her assistants "Malcolm." She claimed she didn't like to be bothered by details such as learning new names all the time. In reality, she was more interested in fostering her reputation as an eccentric, not to mention brilliant, businesswoman. As head of a $370 million international conglomerate, she could be as eccentric as she damned well pleased.

Of all the Malcolms Lucretia had had, she liked this one the best. She also respected him the most, which was more important. But she had absolutely no intention of letting him know that.

"Ready, Malcolm?" She let impatience tinge her tone.

"Absolutely." His calm demeanor was in direct contrast to her high-energy stance.

"Good." She resumed pacing. "My to-do list for July 21." She glanced at him to make sure he was with her. He was, as always.

"First," she said, "our people in Hong Kong are to proceed with the acquisition as planned. Call them and tell them Addison Enterprises is ready to *move.* They would be well advised to act swiftly and decisively. This is not the time to get cold feet."

"Got it." He made a few notes and waited for her to go on.

"Second," she said in the same crisp tone, "I've changed my mind about that diamond tiara Ransom's sent over the other day on approval. I've decided I want it after all. *But...* I want it delivered by the close of business today or it's no sale."

"I'm sure that won't be a problem," he predicted, making notes on his pad.

"That's the spirit, Malcolm. I knew I could count on you."

He nodded, pen poised for directive number three.

When she did not immediately proceed, he glanced up with a question on his face. "Is that all, Lucy?"

"Almost." He was the only employee of Addison Enterprises who called her "Lucy." She wondered why she allowed it. "Last but not least—" She returned to the tinted glass wall and stared out moodily. Time to quit pussyfooting around, she reminded herself. Fortune favors the bold. She who hesitates is lost.

"Last but not least," she repeated in ringing tones, "*I want my daughter married*. And you, dear Malcolm, are going to make that happen."

1

CHARLES LAWRENCE—"Charley" to friends, of whom he had many, but *not* including his boss— stared at said boss. "Say what?" he inquired, hoping he'd misunderstood, but fairly sure he hadn't.

"*I said,* I want my daughter married. Have you developed a hearing problem, Malcolm? What's so hard to understand about that?" Lucretia resumed her pacing. "Sabrina's twenty-five years old, for heaven's sake. She's not getting any younger."

"I got that part," Charley said. "Didn't you tack something else onto the end?"

"Oh, that." She shrugged. "I said, you're going to help me achieve my ends. And you are."

Charley's jaw tightened and he stared at Lucretia, trying to think of a response that would register his strong disapproval and not get him fired. Did she really think—

But of course she did. Lucretia Addison was used to getting every little thing she wanted, whether it be a diamond tiara or some poor unfortunate underling's head on a platter. She was a shark was what she was, although you wouldn't know it to look at her.

She stood before him with her hands on her sleek hips and her expensively coiffed blond head tilted to one side, giving him that familiar challenging stare.

If he didn't know she was one of the most powerful businesswomen in the country and had a twenty-five-year-old daughter, he'd probably think she was somewhere between forty and forty-five. On the other hand, judging by pure orneriness, she'd be about a hundred.

Even so, she was a damned good-looking woman. She worked for it, though. Several times a week her personal trainer came to the Addison Building to put her through her paces in her personal minigymnasium, part of this turquoise-and-buff executive suite. The result was a sleek and toned body with legs that wouldn't quit.

She dressed that body with confidence, favoring bright colors such as the clear red jersey dress she wore today with a triple strand of pearls that probably cost more than the national debt. Okay, maybe that was a slight exaggeration, but Charley was sure they were worth more than enough to buy *his* dream.

His dream. He had to remember his dream and hang on to it. "Look, I really don't know what I could do to help you with your daughter," he said, trying to conceal his exasperation. "I barely know—" He broke off, realizing he'd been about to say "the princess," which was what all the Addison employees called Lucretia's daughter, Sabrina. Hastily he changed course. "Ms. Addison. I have no influence whatsoever."

Lucretia's scarlet lips curved up at the corners even while her blue eyes narrowed. Fingering her pearls with beautifully manicured hands, she perched on the corner of the massive marble desk. Even her shoes matched the image: high red heels that made her feet look long and narrow and elegant.

"All you have to do," she said as if the matter were settled, "is follow instructions. I chose you for this important mission because you *don't* have a history with Sabrina. You can win her trust. You're the kind of sincere young man who—"

The telephone rang. "Hang on a minute, Malcolm." She lifted the receiver and spoke impatiently. "Yes, Marge, what the— Oh. All right, I'll talk to him." She gave Charley a slight shrug that in no way expressed apology and turned away.

He sat there, holding his leather-bound notebook between fingers white with strain. This was not the first time Lucy had tried to get him involved with her personal problems, but he'd always found a way to sidestep. She seemed to think the entire world revolved around what she wanted, both personally and professionally. Who the hell did she think she was, anyway?

And then he realized what a stupid question that was. She knew exactly who she was. And she knew who *he* was, too.

Lucy lived by the Golden Rule: she had the gold Charley needed, so she made the rules. He could like it or lump it.

But if he could just hang on a little longer, he'd have saved enough money to realize his lifelong dream. He could make a triumphant return to Kansas City, where he would open the greatest barbecue restaurant in the continental United States—hell, the best damned barbecue restaurant in the world.

Okay, calm down, he told himself. *Listen to what*

she has to say before throwing yourself on your spear.
Concentrate on the bottom line....

She concluded her telephone call and hung up the receiver. When she looked at him, he thought she seemed at least slightly more cautious in her optimism.

"All right," she said, "this is the deal. Sabrina will be twenty-five years old on August 11 and I'm going to throw the mother of all birthday parties for her. All the guests will be ferried by my yacht to my island off the coast of Santa Barbara, where Sabrina will reign like a princess royal."

Lucretia flung her arms in the air dramatically and waited, apparently expecting him to be impressed.

What he was was relieved. "Sounds good, Lucy, but you don't need me for that." He snapped closed his notebook. "If that's all, I'll make these calls right away and get back to—"

"That's *not* all!" She pointed one of those scary red fingernails. "It's more...complicated than that."

Wasn't it always?

She went on. "As part of the festivities, I plan to trot past my daughter every eligible—and acceptable—bachelor I can dredge up." She accented her determination by pounding a fist into her palm. "I swear by all that's holy, Sabrina will choose one of them or she's never getting off that island!"

"Now, Lucy, you can't—"

"I can and I will." She glared at him. "This is important, Malcolm! If left to her own devices, the girl would probably spend the rest of her life on that...that *farm* in Santa Barbara, getting dirt under her fingernails and communing with nature. It's disgusting."

Charley happened to know "that *farm* in Santa Barbara" was a multimillion-dollar estate given to Sabrina on her twenty-first birthday by the same mother who now protested so bitterly. Nevertheless, being wise to the ways of said mother, he didn't remind her of that fact.

He apparently didn't have to, for she said, "Okay, I know what you're thinking, but you're wrong. It's what *I* think that's important."

"Even so," Charley said dryly, "I'm a bit in the dark here as to how I can help your cause."

She looked astonished. "Didn't I explain all that? There's only one teeny tiny problem with my plan— how to get Bree *on* the island in the first place. After what happened last year—" She sighed dramatically.

Charley wasn't at Sabrina's party last year. But like all Addison employees, he'd heard the whispers: how the birthday girl walked out following a public but mysterious quarrel with her mother. He'd heard the gossip but hadn't participated, knowing the inherent dangers in even the most casual remark being relayed to his hypersensitive boss, who never forgave disloyalty.

What could he have said anyway? Privately, he considered Sabrina Addison a spoiled brat. Every year, her birthday apparently became a bigger and bigger event, until last year's extravaganza, which was practically a coronation.

He remembered what he'd thought when he heard Lucy had rented Disneyland: *Jeez, more money than good sense.* And yet, beneath the scorn, he'd felt...*sorry* for Lucretia Addison because she tried so hard and it still didn't work.

Lucretia gave a disgusted sigh. "All right, there was a little...*situation* last year, but that's all over and done with. This year everything will be different. This year, everything will be *perfect.*"

She paused as if expecting him to respond, so he said a noncommittal, "I don't doubt that for a minute." But he was thinking it was bound to be worse.

That appeared to please her, because she nodded. "So all we—"

He noticed that "we" without pleasure.

"Have to do is get her to attend her own birthday party and I'll take it from there. That's where you come in, dear Malcolm—it's all up to you."

That shocked him out of his self-imposed composure. "How the hell am I supposed to do that?"

"Simple," Lucretia said with a man-eating smile. "You'll lie to her. You'll tell her that her mother's health isn't as good as it appears—" she leaned back on a hand braced on the desktop, raising the other to press dramatically against her forehead "—and if she doesn't show a little consideration I might just fall into a swoon and never recover."

"No way!" Charley surged to his feet indignantly. Thus far he'd kept his sanity, such as it was, by staying out of his employer's personal business. "You can't possibly expect me—"

"Ah, but I do." She pinned him with a steely gaze.

"She'd never go for it. You're the picture of health," he said.

She smiled. "Thank you, dear boy. But looks can be deceiving."

Before his eyes, she seemed to wilt, becoming smaller and suddenly vulnerable. Could she be telling the truth? Could she have some secret medical condition he knew nothing about? She straightened her shoulders, and he saw she was laughing.

That did it. No matter how much he needed this job, he wasn't about to let her jerk him around—

"This little assignment shouldn't be any trouble for such a persuasive young man." Lucretia broke into his hostile thoughts. "Not that I think you can be bought, Malcolm dear, of course not. But to show my gratitude for this little extracurricular chore, there'll be a nice bonus in your paycheck. Just a small token of my gratitude—say, something in the four-figure range…?"

2

SABRINA ADDISON knelt on a foam knee pad at the edge of a patch of seathrift, hardy pink puffballs native to the California coast. Thrusting her fingers into the soft earth, she examined the moisture content of the soil.

"This seems fine, Juan," she called to the man farther down the graveled path. "I don't think we'll need to water again until Thursday."

"I think you're right, *señorita,* as usual. You have a gift for knowing what the gardens need." Even at a distance, the flash of his white teeth was plainly visible in his dark face, as were the streaks of gray in his black hair. "I'll go on down to the lemon groves and check there."

She nodded, standing up and brushing off the knees of her khaki trousers. "That'll be fine. I'll take a look at the rest of the garden, just in case."

"Good idea." He moved away. "The irrigation system is supposed to be fixed, but seeing is believing."

Dear Juan, Sabrina thought with affection, watching him disappear around the corner of the house. He and his wife were direct opposites in temperament, he being unfailingly pessimistic and Teresa being equally unfailingly optimistic. Sabrina, in her own opinion at least, maintained an even keel in all matters, so there was nice balance to life on Rancho El Dorado.

Turning, she surveyed her Spanish-Mediterranean hillside villa with deep satisfaction. Pink stucco gleamed in the afternoon sun and red roof tiles made a pleasant contrast to garden greenery and more distant ocean blue. On a clear day, and this was, the view encompassed not only mountains and ocean, but islands, as well. Surely no more beautiful spot existed than this, nestled in a valley of the coastal mountains of Santa Barbara.

Her mother had thought her mad when Sabrina asked for this place on her twenty-first birthday, but as usual, Sabrina knew what she wanted. Since then she'd bought considerable additional acreage, gradually increasing the organic farming operation until it included not only the existing avocados and citrus but several exotic varieties of fruit and vegetables and many experimental crops.

Juan and Teresa had more or less come with the property, which in retrospect had been as fortuitous as finding the place itself. Sabrina could never begin to repay her foreman for all he'd taught her about this land and what could be coaxed from its heart.

Artemisia and lamb's ears joined with the seathrift, soft texture around the many fountains scattered throughout the gardens. Curving graveled pathways circled the house, meandering through the gardens. Carefully placed benches and boulders offered temptations to linger in search of the peacefulness Sabrina had found when she moved here for good two years ago.

It was she who had planned this garden and Juan who had helped her execute it so brilliantly, teaching her as they went. They made a dynamite team, she thought with satisfaction. Brushing damp bangs away from her forehead, she glanced up at the cloudless sky with a little sigh of pleasure.

Another perfect day in Paradise.

The crunch of footsteps on gravel brought her swinging around toward the house. Teresa was hurrying along the path, carrying a glass of something tall and frosty. Teresa always hurried; fast was her only speed.

"Here, drink this!" she commanded, thrusting the glass forward. "Lemonade made from your own lemons—it's good!"

"Thanks, Teresa." Bree accepted the glass and drank deeply. "Delicious."

Teresa shrugged, suddenly modest. "We don't want you getting dehydrated!"

"Not a chance."

"Hey, somebody's got to look out for you!" Teresa always spoke in exclamatory sentences. "You don't do such a hot job on your own!"

"Now you sound like my mother," Bree said wryly.

Teresa quickly crossed herself. "Heaven protect us!"

Bree laughed. "Exactly. But thanks anyway." She handed over the now-empty glass.

"So what you doin' now? You going into town?"

"Why should I go into town?" Bree asked calmly. "I have everything I need right here."

"That's what you think!" Teresa rolled her eyes

expressively. "I thought that nice Mr. Wells invited you to—"

"Matchmaking again, Teresa?"

"I never would!" The housekeeper looked properly indignant at the very idea. "It's just that—well, it's unnatural, a girl your age living here all alone day after day, month after—"

"Woman. I'm a woman. I haven't been a girl in years."

"That's what you think—" Teresa halted mid-sentence to cock her head toward the front of the house, which was shielded by trees and shrubbery. "Somebody's coming."

"Oh, bother!" Sabrina had managed to forget that her mother was sending someone out with papers to be signed. The disruption in her usual quiet routine almost made her wish she'd refused all those gifts of Addison stock over the years. Still, she wouldn't kill the messenger.

She glanced down at herself in her working clothes: khaki trousers, a white T-shirt, dirt-smudged sneakers. A scarf was holding her long hair back, and she must look a sight.

Unfortunately, there wasn't time to make herself presentable without keeping her caller waiting. "Relax, Teresa. It's just Mother's messenger. I'll take care of it."

"I don't suppose we'll have an extra for dinner." Teresa sounded hopeful.

"No."

"Too bad. You live like a hermit. It'd be nice to have a guest for once." Shaking her head, Teresa charged back toward her kitchen while Sabrina squared her shoulders and went to greet her visitor.

CHARLEY COULDN'T believe he'd let Lucy talk him into doing this. The whole ninety miles north from the city, he'd castigated himself mercilessly for being an idiot.

Not that he hadn't made the trip before on his employer's behalf; he had, many times. But this time was different.

Even so, he got the usual feeling of unreality when he drove between the towering Santa Ynez Mountains to his right and the Pacific Ocean on his left. Sheltered between these two geographical features, Santa Barbara basked in sunshine and a lush tropical atmosphere year-round. For a native midwesterner, none of this seemed real.

La-La Land, Charley thought grumpily, turning off Highway 101. Here, the coastline ran from east to west instead of north to south, as it should have. Everything was backward. Hell, on the west coast the sun should set over the ocean, but Santa Barbara, the Oz of America, couldn't even get that right.

The road he turned onto led away from the beach and up a narrow mountain road. As he drove higher, he passed through avocado and lemon groves, crossed a couple of creeks and entered a beautiful valley of oak woodlands. The house, he knew, was perched on the highest spot on the side of the valley overlooking the ocean. He drove toward it, fighting nameless feelings.

It had never seemed right to him that one not-very-

old, not-very-bright, much-too-beautiful rich babe
owned all this.

He drove through massive stone gates, beneath a
hanging sign that declared this to be Rancho El Dorado. Rounding a corner, he saw the house. As always, its sheer size and majesty took his breath away.

Sabrina Addison's playground had it all: views of
ocean and mountains, stone terraces and fabulous gardens, a swimming pool and tennis courts and God
only knows what else. Here she lived like royalty,
queen of all she surveyed, alone like a princess in a
tower of her own creation.

She appeared from around a corner of the house
and he forgot what he'd been thinking. Hell, he forgot
his name and, for a blessed second, why he was even
here.

Sabrina Addison was drop-dead gorgeous. A beautiful princess in a tower—

Long, light-brown hair swung in satin ribbons past
her shoulders, and was held in place by some kind of
scarf the exact color of the skies. Big, brown eyes,
slightly slanted beneath long, lash-brushing bangs,
peered out of a perfectly oval face. A smudge of dirt
adorned one high cheekbone, giving her beauty a desperately needed touch of reality.

But those lips—Charley swallowed convulsively.
Those lips always haunted him for days after he saw
them. They were so full and soft and...vulnerable.
For all her money and privileges, he saw a...a *need-
iness* in Sabrina Addison's mouth that ripped his heart
out.

Or would have, if he'd let it, if he hadn't known it

was nothing more than illusion. He was confident that like her mother, she needed nothing and no one.

Face aside, the rest of her wasn't bad, either: long slim legs in khaki, a T-shirt lightly molding delightfully generous breasts. Her arms beneath the short knit sleeves were a light golden shade, which spoke of hours lolling beside the pool or volleying balls around the tennis court with the rest of the idle rich.

But there was no time for such thoughts now; he had to put on his game face. Charley Lawrence had a job to do and he'd do it—if he could just figure out how the hell to go about it.

Sabrina approached the car with what looked like a cautious smile of greeting. He climbed out to meet her, lugging his bulging briefcase with him. The heat surprised him, once he was outside the air-conditioned car. He felt sweat trickle between his shoulder blades and wished he'd taken off his suit jacket before he left Los Angeles.

Sabrina smiled just for him and he felt it all the way down to his toes. Damn, she was gorgeous. Maybe he'd misjudged her. Maybe he'd—

She spoke. "Hello, Malcolm. Lucretia said you'd be dropping by."

Malcolm. She was just as bad as her mother. Neither one of them knew who the hell he really was.

MALCOLM WAS IMPOSSIBLE to read, Sabrina reflected, leading him to a shady flagstone terrace overlooking mountains sloping down to the sea. He always puzzled her because she never saw on his face the admiration she was accustomed to receiving from the male sex.

Actually, she never saw *anything* on his face. He played everything so close to the vest that she had no idea what he was really thinking, what he was really like.

Good looking, though. She slanted him a cool glance, admiring the shape of his face, noticing the attractive creases in his cheeks that suggested laughter was not completely unknown to him, although his was to her. She liked the smooth way his hair waved away from a neat side part. Even the glasses were attractive, although they made him look even more serious and businesslike, if that was possible.

Almost before they were seated at a wrought-iron-and-glass patio table, Teresa was there with a cold pitcher of lemonade and a plate of freshly baked cookies. She served them with many sly smiles directed at Malcolm, then withdrew, shaking off Bree's thanks with a brisk, *"¡Qué nada!"*

Malcolm didn't say a word, just took a gulp of his lemonade and stared out at the panorama of sea and sky. His expression, however, didn't change; he might just as well have been looking at a brick wall as at one of the most fabulous views on the entire Pacific coast.

Sabrina rested her elbows on the table and leaned forward. "So," she said, "Lucretia has sent papers for me to sign?"

"That is correct." Malcolm picked up the briefcase on the stones beside him. Unsnapping the latch, he extracted the documents and placed them before her. "If you need time to read these—"

"Not at all," she said. "Have you a pen?"

He nearly frowned. "Do you sign everything that's put before you without reading it?"

She blinked in surprise. That sounded almost... critical. "No," she said, "but if I can't trust my mother, who can I trust?" She gave a slightly bitter little laugh. When he failed to respond in kind, she said more lightly, "Hey, I'm sure it's nothing more than six weeks' worth of quarterly reports."

Now *he* was the one who blinked, thick lashes sweeping down over sea-blue eyes. "Six weeks' worth of—"

"It's a joke, Malcolm," she said gently. "I'm putting you on." She held out her hand. "A pen, please."

He opened his jacket and pulled a fancy gold number from an inside pocket, then offered it to her. She took it, but didn't immediately turn to the papers before her.

"Uh...Malcolm?"

"Yes, Ms. Addison?"

"You must be warm in that jacket. Why not take it and your tie off and get...you know, comfortable?"

She fully expected him to refuse; Malcolm never let down his guard with her. At least she'd done her duty as a good hostess and made the offer. If he preferred to sit there sweltering in July heat—

"Thanks," he said. "I believe I will."

To her astonishment, he did. There was something so sexy about the way he peeled off his jacket that she quickly averted her eyes and began to sign her name beside each little yellow-flagged line.

By the time she finished, he looked like a different man minus the coat and tie; it was as if she'd never seen him before. His throat, she saw, was strong and brown, rising from the opened collar of his dress shirt. He'd unbuttoned his cuffs and rolled up his sleeves, displaying muscular forearms and a watch with all kinds of dials and displays on a heavy leather band.

While he was at it, he'd removed his glasses and placed them on the table before him. She stared, resisting the urge to say, "Why, Malcolm, without your glasses you're...you're beautiful!" Because he was. She'd had no idea he was so good-looking.

It had been a long time since she'd found a man as attractive as she found this one. Of course, he was only good old Malcolm, her mother's current man Friday. Still, when she pushed back the papers she felt suddenly breathless.

"There," she said. "Signed, sealed and delivered."

It was his cue to take the papers and run along, only he didn't. He just gave her one of those cool glances and said, "Thank you." He didn't stand up, or indeed, make any preparations to leave.

This was never the way their meetings went. She frowned. "So how was the drive up here?" In California, people always talked about traffic, before they got around to the weather.

"Not bad," he said.

Allll righty. He hadn't taken that hint, so she gave him another. "At least the weather's nice. It'll probably still be daylight when you get back to L.A."

He shrugged noncommittally, then looked around at the greenery ringing the patio. "What do you do here?" he asked.

"I—why I—" Surprised, she frowned. "What do you mean, what do I *do* here?"

He gave her that calm, noncommittal glance again. "I mean, what do you grow and why do you grow it? Like all those lemons I saw on my way up here— what becomes of them?"

She relaxed. "Oh, that. We sell them, of course. After paying my workers, I give the profit to a shelter for women and children."

"I see," he said.

He didn't look as if he did, though. Usually when people heard about that, they fell all over her with approval.

When he didn't, she went on less confidently. "We also grow a lot of our own food, and quite a few exotics—macadamia nuts, kiwi, cheremoya, papayas, bananas, that sort of thing."

"Who's 'we'?"

"Me and my workers, but mostly Juan Lopez. Juan's a genius about growing things. He's really the boss when it comes to horticulture. That was his wife, Teresa, who brought the lemonade. Between them, they pretty much run Rancho El Dorado."

"While you play lady farmer?"

"Malcolm," she said, aghast, "I don't *play*."

"I stand corrected." He picked up his glasses and repositioned them on his nose, a subtle veiling of those beautiful eyes. "You enjoy being a lady farmer?"

Was that a note of incredulity she heard? Surely not. "Of course I like it," she assured him warmly. "If I didn't, I wouldn't do it. I feel as if I'm doing something…something important."

"Such as?"

"Contributing to the welfare of the planet." She gave a self-conscious little laugh. She was never asked to explain herself like this and found it difficult to put her feelings into words. "How we raise our food has an enormous effect on our personal, social and environmental health," she explained earnestly. "The harvest of our orchards and fields yields dozens of varieties of fruits and vegetables nearly year-round. Some we sell, some we give away, but all is shared with other citizens of the world. It's as if—" She paused for breath, carried away by her own rhetoric. "It's as if we're giving back some of what we've taken—"

At last his indifferent facade cracked and the disbelief she saw on his face brought her to a stumbling stop. Sheepishly she suggested, "Cliché?"

"Yeah," he admitted, "but in the best traditions of political correctness."

"Thank heaven for that!" Laughing at herself, she stood, determined to bring this uncomfortable session to a close. All the other times he'd come on her mother's behest, she'd offered him food and drink, and each time he'd refused. The lemonade was as close as he'd ever come to accepting hospitality and she noticed he hadn't touched the cookies.

But enough was enough. "Can I offer you anything else before you go?" she asked, determined to bring this meeting to a conclusion. "Another drink... dinner? If not, I'm sure you're getting anxious to—"

"Dinner," he interrupted, "would be nice. If it's

not too much trouble, of course."

"Oh, no, certainly not," she said, stunned. "I'll just find Teresa and give her the...uh...good news."

3

"YOU'RE KIDDING!" Teresa peered past Bree's shoulder at the man sitting at the patio table beneath the shade of a bright-orange umbrella. "He's staying for dinner?"

"Teresa!" Bree, tempted to stamp her foot, pursed her lips, instead. "I'm allowed to have guests to dinner, aren't I?"

"Sure," Teresa agreed airily, "you just never do." Her dark eyes gleamed. "'Specially not somebody who works for *la patrona*."

Bree spared a quick glance at her "guest." Beneath his pale-blue shirt, his shoulders looked extraordinarily wide. "I couldn't help it," she whispered sharply at her troublesome housekeeper. "I was just being polite when I invited him, and he took me up on it."

Teresa shrugged. "Hey, I don't care why. I'm just glad to have someone besides you to cook for. You eat like a bird, little girl. So what do you want me to cook?"

"I don't care—a salad? Something fast so I can get him out of here."

"So what important matters demand your immediate attention?"

"Well...Juan said he had some new seed catalogs for me to look at."

Teresa let out an explosive sigh. "You'd rush through dinner with a cute guy so you can look at seeds with an old, married man? Bree, you've got a screw loose!"

"Teresa, go cook!" But she added a plaintive, "Please?"

Teresa went with much harrumphing. Dredging up a smile, Bree returned to Malcolm. "We'll have dinner soon," she promised. "In the meantime, would you care for a drink? Wine, a cocktail—whatever you'd like." She was sure he wouldn't take her up on that invitation. She'd never known Malcolm to drink alcohol, and with a drive back to the city ahead of him—

"Thank you," he said. "I would like a drink."

She tried not to show her surprise or her disappointment. "Wh-why, certainly. What would you—"

"What are you having?"

She hadn't intended to have anything; she was just being polite. "I guess I'll have champagne," she said without enthusiasm.

"I'll have the same."

"I'll get the wine, then." She rose to her feet.

He stood up, too, making her feel smaller and more delicate than she was. "I'll help you."

"No need—"

He followed her anyway so she stifled her protests. From the refrigerator behind the wet bar in the family room, she considered the possibilities: something nice without being ostentatious, neither too cheap nor too expensive. Selecting a bottle from those arrayed inside, she turned and found him so close that she gasped in reaction.

It was as if he'd stepped forward at just the wrong—or right—time. She found herself only inches away from being in his arms. She gave him a bewildered smile and stepped back, clutching the bottle with both hands. "I beg your pardon! I didn't mean—"

"No harm done," he said quickly. "May I open that for you?"

She surrendered the bottle and turned to choose two flutes while he did the honors. When amber liquid bubbled in fragile crystal, she lifted hers in a salute.

"What shall we toast?" she asked lightly.

"A good crop?"

Surely he wasn't laughing at her. "That's nice, but it would only apply to me," she protested, deciding to take his words at face value. "How about…" She chewed her lip for a moment. "To a pleasant summer?"

He scowled. "My hopes aren't very high in that regard. How about…" His lovely blue eyes narrowed. "To our loved ones?"

She had no idea why he'd said that, but good manners prevailed. "To our loved ones, whoever and wherever they may be."

They sipped. She gave him a warmly approving smile. "While we're waiting, would you care to see the gardens? They're quite pleasant, especially in the evening shade."

"I'd like that very much," he agreed with alacrity. "After you, m'lady."

She had no idea why he'd said *that,* but it seemed somehow charming. With a nod of acquiescence, she sailed past to lead him to her pride and joy. Whether or not he enjoyed it, she knew *she* would. It was her green thumb, as much as Juan's know-how, that had produced such abundance.

WHETHER OR NOT she enjoyed steering him around her lavish estate, Charley enjoyed seeing the efforts of the hired help. And he enjoyed seeing *her*. Sabrina Addison was a babe, albeit a rich, spoiled, shallow, underworked, overprotected—

She stopped in the path ahead of him and turned, cocking her head to look at him with a question on her beautiful face. The long, shining hair swooped over her shoulders as if carefully arranged there for maximum effect, although she hadn't so much as touched it.

"I'm sorry?" he said blankly. "Did you say something?"

"I said, here in Santa Barbara they call this style of landscape design 'Mission Japanese.' I thought you'd find that...I don't know, kind of funny?"

"Right," he agreed, still in the dark. "Funny. What does it mean, exactly?"

She flipped that shimmery veil of silken hair back with a toss of her head. "Who knows? It's just a tag for elements of Spanish Mission and Japanese styles, plus a dash of New Mexico and the Southwest, with a few dry tropical aspects thrown in for good measure."

He didn't have a clue what she was talking about. He wondered if she did and decided she didn't, that she was probably parroting what some expensive landscape gardener had told her. He nodded—he hoped wisely. "Sounds reasonable," he declared. "To repeat myself, what does it mean?"

She laughed; she had a beautiful, musical laugh. "It means nothing too square or too flat or too noisy."

"Noisy plants?"

"You'd be surprised." She gestured with a graceful arm. "Everything has its own space, including people. The plant groupings are allowed to naturally size and contour themselves with only minor shaping. This kind of garden is easy to care for and doesn't use much water...."

She almost sounded as if she knew what she was talking about. With an occasional wise "Uh-huh," Charley followed her along the meandering walkways, past fountains and benches and views that must have added a few extra million to the cost of this place.

She paused on a rise overlooking the sky-blue swimming pool, glittering in the fading sunlight like a jewel. Below them, Teresa went about setting the patio table for their meal, working from a rolling cart that contained silver, crystal, linen, an arrangement of roses....

Sabrina smiled at him. "I love my gardens," she said in a dreamy voice. "I think we all need a feeling of...of *space* and *peace* in our cluttered lives, don't you?"

Charley Lawrence, who'd grown up between orphanages and foster homes and who hadn't known what "peace" was until he was old enough to vote, nodded seriously. "Absolutely," he agreed.

Her smile indicated warm approval. "I felt sure

you'd understand," she said. "Shall we go down and see how Teresa's doing with dinner?"

"After you."

He gave her a cynical little bow, thinking he should be ashamed of himself. But then he realized that the gentlewoman farmer seemed to appreciate it.

NO SOONER WERE THEY seated than Teresa wheeled out her little cart with a cargo of guacamole and salsa and corn chips. There was also a big pitcher of frozen margaritas and two glasses with the traditional flaring bowls. Sabrina tried not to let her impatience show.

This did *not* look like a prelude to a simple salad meal.

Teresa served the drinks, grinning at Malcolm. "How's it going?" she asked. "*La patrona* still drivin' you *loco?*" She winked broadly.

Malcolm grinned back with dazzling effect. Sabrina blinked in shock. Somehow she hadn't thought Malcolm capable of smiling. He ought to do it more often. Or maybe not.

"*¡Sí!*" he said to Teresa.

Sabrina joined in the general laughter over that response. "Poor Malcolm," she said sympathetically.

His "Amen!" sounded heartfelt.

He reached for a chip and dipped it into the guacamole, but instead of popping it into his mouth, he looked it over carefully. "You make this?" he asked Teresa.

She nodded proudly. "Taste it," she urged. "It's good stuff."

He did, and Sabrina found herself watching him

chew with a sensual pleasure she could almost feel.
She swallowed hard and looked away.

"It *is* good," he agreed, licking his lips. "The salsa
is..."

"Secret recipe," Teresa informed him. She
watched him look it over, then swirl a chip through.
"You're not by any chance a cook yourself?" she
asked, sounding suspicious.

He paused with the chip halfway to his mouth,
seeming to consider. Then he said, "Not exactly."
He slipped the chip and its juicy tomato topping past
his lips, chewed with appreciation, swallowed. "Sort
of," he amended. "Not really."

"Well, which is it?" Teresa demanded. "Either
you are or—"

"Teresa, don't you have something you should be
doing in the kitchen?" Sabrina interrupted. She
couldn't let the woman harass her guest this way,
even if he was her mother's proxy. "We're just
having a simple salad, but I'm sure you'll enjoy it,"
she added for his benefit.

"Changed the menu." Teresa looked miffed by her
dismissal.

"But—"

"Have I ever poisoned you, Sabrina Addison?
You'll eat what I serve you!"

Teresa flounced away. Sabrina sighed. "I apologize
for that," she said, lifting her gaze to meet Malcolm's. "Now I don't know *what* we're having, but
I'm sure it will be delicious."

"It doesn't matter," he said.

He was doing such a good job on the chips and
dips that she had to wonder when he'd last eaten.

Somehow that endeared him to her in some impersonal way. He was, after all, a big boy.

The steady movement of his hand between his mouth and the food slowed, then stopped. He looked somehow uncomfortable all at once. He reached for his margarita and took a bracing gulp.

"Uhhh...Sabrina, there's something I need to—"

"Fajitas!" Teresa burst upon them again, pushing her cart ahead of her. A huge cast-iron skillet sizzled, fragrant steam rising from strips of meat. Bowls of condiments and a covered tortilla warmer were also on hand.

Cheerfully Teresa unloaded her bounty. Then she rocked back on her heels, hands on her hips.

"Good stuff, Malcolm!" she said with strident confidence, indicating the combination of charbroiled strips of flank steak and chicken breast, surrounded by sautéed onions, tomatoes and green peppers with sides of sour cream, more guacamole and *pico de gallo.* "Made the tortillas, too. You won't find anything like that in a *restaurant!*"

Sabrina shifted uneasily in her padded chair. "Malcolm, you were saying...?"

"Teresa, I suspect there are unplumbed depths to your talents," Malcolm said, not paying any attention at all to Sabrina. "Do you do *carnitas?*"

"Do I do *carnitas! Does* a bear—"

"Teresa!" Sabrina exclaimed.

The woman looked offended. "Sleep in the woods? You like *carnitas,* Malcolm?"

"It's barbecue. I like anything that's barbecued."

"No kiddin'." Teresa looked around, spotted another chair nearby and pulled it forward. "You let me know the next time you're comin' and I'll—"

"*Teresa!*"

Both of them looked at Sabrina as if she'd lost her mind. She managed a calm smile. "Thank you," she said graciously. "We can take it from here."

"But—"

"Teresa, if you want to invite Malcolm to visit you, feel free to do so." All she wanted at this point was to get this over with so he'd go, and here Teresa was creating one delay after another.

"Good idea!" Teresa stood up. "We'll check our calendars." With a wink for Malcolm, she departed.

Sabrina heaved a sigh of relief. "As you were saying, Malcolm..."

"Later, okay?" He lifted the lid to the tortilla warmer and extracted a round disk, its white surface spotted with dark grill marks. He began heaping on meat, tomatoes, onions, guacamole—

Sabrina watched him and sighed. She had the very strong feeling that she was on the verge of discovering the key to his very peculiar behavior. Well, she could wait if she must...although waiting wasn't one of her best things.

She reached for a tortilla of her own, then stopped short with it balanced on her open palm. Teresa had brought only one enormous skillet containing enough food for a half-dozen people; they were obviously expected to share.

For some reason, that struck her as entirely too intimate. This was their first meal together, after all. She glanced at him with a frown, but he was totally concentrating on his food.

She chuckled to herself; she was being silly.

Obviously Malcolm had no interest in her whatsoever. This was quite unusual, but he was, after all, an employee of her mother's. She must not make him feel uncomfortable or inferior in any way. Squaring her shoulders, she plucked a sliver of chicken from the skillet and laid it carefully on her tortilla.

Malcolm laughed; he actually laughed. "You'll starve to death that way," he said, sounding almost as if he was teasing her. "Here, let me help."

Taking her fork from her unresisting hand, he began to pile chicken and beef on her tortilla, while she watched in something akin to horror. She didn't want all this. She didn't want him to take it upon himself—

He lifted a final choice bit of meat and paused, frowning at her overflowing tortilla. Apparently realizing that one more morsel would very likely send an avalanche down the mountain, he shrugged and lifted it to her lips instead.

And she, unwillingly, parted her lips to receive it.

THIS WAS GETTING out of hand, Charley realized. If he didn't say his piece and say it fast, he wasn't going to say it at all. Dropping the fork onto her plate, he sat back in his chair.

"Sabrina, I think it's time I told you why—"

"Oh, Malcolm, why don't you let that wait until we finish dinner? You said yourself that was best." She sounded almost petulant.

Five minutes ago, *she* was the one trying to get him to talk. Now she wanted to eat? He watched her maneuver her tortilla from hand to plate, feeling torn.

Lucy hadn't done him any favors sending him here. If he got out of this alive—

"Dessert, everybody!"

Teresa stopped short, holding a colorful pottery bowl in one hand and a plate of cookies in the other. She frowned. "You going to eat, or you just going to sit there staring at each other?"

Charley couldn't believe it, but a becoming shade of rose swept up to cover Sabrina's aristocratic cheekbones. She was actually blushing. Hastily she reached for her fork.

Teresa harrumphed again, deposited the bowl and plate on the cart and flounced away. Feeling almost sorry for Sabrina, which didn't make any sense at all, Charley asked between bites, "So how did you get interested in...farming?"

She brightened. "It just sort of happened. I came to Rancho El Dorado the first time with a friend who was thinking about buying it. He wasn't impressed. It was kind of rundown and needed a lot of work, but I fell in love with it." She smiled suddenly. "I met Juan and Teresa that day, too. When Lucretia gave me this place for my twenty-first birthday, they more or less came with it."

At the word "birthday," Charley felt a stab of guilt. "That was nice of your mother," he said, trying to encourage filial feelings.

It didn't appear to be working. "I suppose," Sabrina said carelessly. "Anyway, with the help of Juan and Teresa, I started restoring the place to its former glory, you might say. Along the way I discovered that I really do have a knack for growing things."

Or maybe it was a knack for hiring people who

knew what they're doing. Must be genetic, Charley thought. But what he said was, "Really?"

She nodded, apparently reading nothing into the single word. "I've bought more land since then, and we've planted new crops. We can grow anything. We have what's called a frost-free microclimate."

"A what?"

She nodded, looking enormously pleased. "We're ninety-nine percent frost-free, with artesian spring water and year-round sunshine. We use organic methods and have been expanding our olive and avocado and lemon orchards by adding peaches, cheremoya, mandarins and plums.... We grow more than a hundred varieties of fruits and veggies and we're harvesting something almost year-round."

She continued with a passion he'd never seen in her before. "Not only that, we provide homes for so much wildlife. We've got hawks, rabbits, even an occasional bobcat. We've worked so hard to restore the creek and small riparian wetland, to protect the land—"

She stopped short, seeming to realize all at once that she was leaning earnestly over the table and staring into his eyes. Hers were brown and as soft as velvet and if he didn't hang on, he'd find himself adrift in them.

She caught her breath sharply. "I'm doing it again, aren't I?"

"Doing what?"

"Taking clichés and political correctness to new heights."

He smiled in spite of himself. "Well, apparently you put your money where your mouth is," he said.

"Are you the one who named this place El Dorado or did it come that way?"

She looked a bit sheepish. "I named it, or actually, *re*named it. The last owners called it 'Hidden Acres Farm.' I thought it deserved better." She wrinkled her nose in an appealing grimace.

"I agree," he said softly. "El Dorado—the golden one. I'd say that's appropriate."

She nodded eagerly. "Especially at this time of day." She gestured toward the ocean below, the mountains behind which the sun was lowering. The final rays of the day spilled over Rancho El Dorado, gilding everything they touched, especially the woman.

She looked like a golden goddess sitting there.

A beautiful, rich, golden goddess from whom he wanted something of critical importance to his career and, indeed, his very life.

He cleared his throat. "Sabrina…there's something I have to ask you."

"There is?" She turned her face toward him with a smooth, graceful motion. Her eyes glowed with uncharted depths; her breasts rose with a quick intake of breath. "I feel so close to you at this moment, Malcolm. You really seem to understand how I feel. So go ahead, what is it you want to ask me?"

"Well, it's…" He sucked in a deep breath and said all in a rush, "Your-mother-wants-to-give-you-a-fabulous-birthday-party-but-she's-afraid-you-won't-come."

He saw her eyes go wide as if with shock and he caught himself up short, then continued in a more controlled voice. "She sent me to plead her case with you, Sabrina. Will you go to your birthday party and make your mother incredibly happy or..."

Or will you act like a spoiled brat and break your mother's heart?

Although unspoken, the thought was there. He knew she heard it echoing in his mind.

SHE'D THOUGHT he was going to—what? Ask her to go to the prom? To a movie? What was she, some silly kid who thought he was dazzled by *her* and not by who she was?

This wasn't the first time Lucretia had sent someone to do her dirty work. It was just that Sabrina had thought Malcolm might be...different. Better. She slumped in her chair, and a familiar sense of disappointment swept over her.

"Well?" he asked. "Will you go to your own birthday party, Sabrina?"

She shook her head slowly, her teeth clamped over her bottom lip to control its trembling.

"Now, don't be too hasty." He fidgeted in his chair. "What could it hurt? This means a lot to her."

"I'm well aware of that," Sabrina said bitterly. "Having her own way always means a lot to her."

"You've got her all wrong."

Poor Malcolm, she thought without sympathy. Why did this mean so much to *him?* He was just doing his job. "I know her better than you do," she reminded him after a moment.

"Sure you do, but you didn't see her. She's got big plans for a real gala event. All she asks—"

"Is to control me and everybody else around her, body and soul." Sabrina kept shaking her head. "I can't let her keep doing this to me—I swore I wouldn't! I'm trying desperately to make my own way, to stand on my own two feet. I can't let her keep sweeping into my life and tearing everything apart.''

Malcolm grimaced. ''It's not like that, honest. She wants to do this for *you,* not for herself. She wants to give you the mother of all birthday parties—her exact words. All she asks is that you show up.''

Sabrina closed her eyes and let her head slump forward. ''Do you really believe what you're saying? That isn't nearly all she's asking.''

''It is, Sabrina. She wants to throw you a bash to end all bashes. We're talking house party, Addison Island, yachts, jewels, balls—hell, d'you want TV coverage? She'll do that, too. She's prepared to move heaven and earth to make everything up to you.''

''Make *what* up to me?'' Sabrina asked quickly, suspiciously.

He shrugged; he was beginning to look a little ragged around the edges, now that they'd finally gotten down to brass tacks. ''Whatever,'' he said, a note of desperation entering his voice. ''Your mother doesn't confide *everything* in me. I don't know what she did to upset you so much that you'd refuse to go to your own birthday party, but whatever it was, she's ready to go to the mat to fix it.''

''You're wrong. She just wants to be in control. That's all she ever wants.'' Sabrina lifted her chin, blinking back tears. ''I can't let her do that any longer. You don't know what I've been through. You don't know....''

Now it was his turn to sigh. ''No,'' he said, ''I don't know and I don't want to know. I didn't want to do this." He sliced one hand through the air. "I told her it wouldn't work, but she insisted."

"She's manipulating you, too," Sabrina observed sadly. "She's controlling you. You shouldn't let her get away with it, Malcolm."

He stood up abruptly. "Of course she controls me," he said with barely controlled impatience. "She's my employer. That's what employers do."

She followed him toward the corner of the house, beyond which lay the graveled sweep of driveway. "But she has no right!" she exclaimed, feeling a responsibility to show him the error of his thinking. "You should tell her—"

He stopped short and turned toward her. "I don't tell *her*—she tells me. She pays for that privilege. As long as what she asks me to do isn't immoral or illegal, I'll do it to the best of my ability—or take a hike. Those are my choices."

"But—"

"But now I've got to get back to the office."

"It's eight o'clock at night! Surely she doesn't expect you to go back to work at this hour."

He shrugged, dropping his suit coat in the process. They bent at the same moment to pick it up and found themselves face-to-face, foreheads nearly touching. Sabrina yanked back, catching her breath on a little note of surprise.

Malcolm didn't bat an eye, just picked up the coat and straightened. "Lucy's waiting at the office, said she'd be there no matter what time I got back. Does that tell you how much this means to her?"

"It tells me she's determined to meddle," Bree said doggedly, lifting her chin to a defiant angle.

"Haven't you heard what I've been trying to tell you?"

For a long moment he met her gaze, his own emotionless. Then he shrugged. "After you said no and made me believe it, I quit listening," he said. "Bye, Ms. Addison. Thanks for dinner and the tour. I'll give your mother your regrets."

"Thank *you*," she said, determined to be courteous to the end, no matter what. "Drop by again any time you're in the neighborhood."

"Yeah, right," he said.

It was a formality and they both knew it.

HE COULDN'T get over it, the way she'd made such a seamless transition from her "lady of the manor" mode to her "tragic princess" mode. He stewed about her performance all the way down the coast to Los Angeles.

Was there a real Sabrina Addison beneath all that posing and role playing and political correctness? Did she have any strongly held, deeply felt opinions about anything except her mother's perfidy?

Okay, Lucretia would never be mistaken for Mother Teresa, but she deserved credit for one thing: love of family. She'd walk on hot coals for her spoiled and ungrateful...and beautiful...daughter.

Charley berated himself for responding to Sabrina's beauty and that sense of vulnerability, but he responded anyway. His self-condemnation wasn't because he thought she was so far above him socially, which she was, or economically, which she was. It was because he didn't sense any substance in her.

Charley Lawrence liked women of substance,

which was probably why he'd stuck it out with Lucretia Addison as long as he had. Whether you liked the woman or not, she had the guts of a bullfighter and the determination of—hell, of the little engine that could. Lucretia Addison didn't step aside for anything or anybody. If she'd lived a hundred years earlier, she'd have been a gunfighter.

Since she lived today, she was generally acknowledged to be a bitch. Charley was reluctant to admit he actually *liked* her, but he did. And he sure as hell respected her.

Nevertheless, on the ride up to the penthouse office in the Addison Building, Charley reminded himself that Sabrina was dangerous to his mental health; every time he saw her he had a harder time getting her out of his mind than he'd had the time before. Today had been the worst; they'd almost had a real conversation. If he ever discovered she had a brain as well as a body and an appealing air of helplessness, he'd be doomed.

Lucy would just have to understand. He'd carried out this asinine assignment to the best of his ability, and he'd failed, but that shouldn't surprise her. She was desperate or she'd never have sent him off on such a Mission Impossible in the first place.

At the penthouse door, he straightened his tie, slicked back his hair with both hands and put on his glasses. Before he could reach for the doorknob, the door swung open in his face and Lucretia stood there, wild-eyed and breathing fire.

4

"ALL RIGHT, what happened?" Lucretia demanded. She grabbed Charley's arm and dragged him inside her suite of offices. "Why didn't you turn on the cell phone in the car? I've been going crazy here."

"I forgot," he lied.

"Never mind that now." She released her hold on him. "Is she coming or do I have to play hardball? No, I don't mean that, not with my own child." She looked around wildly. "Damn it, at a time like this I wish I still smoked."

"Smoking will kill you," Charley said.

"*I'll* kill you if you don't tell me what happened." Her eyes flashed. "She's coming!" She said it explosively. "She's coming—I can tell just by looking at you. She's coming, right, Malcolm?"

"She's not coming."

"But— Of course she is. You talked her into it."

"I *tried* to talk her into it. She wasn't buying."

"Malcolm, I counted on you!" It was an anguished wail from a woman always in control.

Charley had had just about enough of this. He was tired, nerves already frayed by the daughter, and in no shape to joust with the mother. "I gave it my best shot."

"Well!" She drew herself up, the Dragon Lady once more. "Your best wasn't good enough."

"Then fire me." He couldn't believe he'd said that; he sure as hell didn't want to put ideas in her head.

She apparently didn't believe he meant it, for she laughed. "Don't be an idiot," she said. "This is no time for a falling out among…"

"Thieves, Lucy. The word you're looking for is *thieves*."

"Certainly not." She glared at him indignantly. "The word I'm looking for is—" She considered for a moment. "*Coconspirators?* No, too political." She frowned. "Help me out here, Malcolm. I'm too stunned by your failure to think straight."

Charley felt suddenly very, very tired. His shoulders slumped. "Look, I'm sorry. I did my best. It wasn't good enough."

"Surely it didn't take six hours for you to extract a simple no," she countered, reverting to her usual acid tone. "Tell me exactly what happened."

He shrugged. "She invited me to stay for dinner, so I did. When I found a way to bring it up—"

"That's good, looking for the perfect moment."

"Don't grasp at straws," he suggested dryly. "She wasn't buying."

Lucretia frowned. "Maybe you didn't put it the right way. Maybe—"

"Maybe I was the wrong one to send on this *mission!*"

"No, no." She waved that aside. "So what did she say, exactly?"

"That she's not going to let you control and manipulate her anymore."

Lucretia gasped. "She said that? How could she be so cruel, so heartless?"

"I got the feeling it was easy." Charley looked longingly at the door. He was dead tired. Tension did that to him. "Look, I'm going home," he announced. "I tried, I failed, end of story."

"No, dear boy." Lucretia's face took on that determined expression that always boded ill for somebody. "You tried, you failed, you'll try again. Tomorrow."

"Forget it." Charley backed away. "Get another errand boy."

"Errand boy! Is that what you think I consider you to be? Nothing could be further from the truth." She advanced on him with determination. "Malcolm, you are a treasured member of my personal staff. Sabrina is the most important thing in the world to me. Do you think I'd send an *errand boy* to deal with her? Never! I need a person of integrity, a person of high moral fiber, someone who wouldn't see this as an opportunity to take advantage of the poor little rich girl—you didn't, did you?"

Charley choked on a denial.

"Of course you wouldn't," she agreed, trapping him between the wall and a leather couch. She laid her hand on his shoulder with an intensity reminiscent of the jaws of life. "That's why I chose you. That's why we must work together to convince my darling but stubborn child—"

"Wonder where she gets that," Charley muttered.

"You'd be surprised," she surprised him by saying. "It's you and me, kid. Sabrina's future—her entire life—hangs in the balance here. If I'm not mistaken—'' she gripped his shoulder so tightly that he winced ''—you're a man of honor who'd never turn his back on a damsel in distress.''

''Your daughter is hardly a damsel in distress.''

''How would you know? As a matter of fact, I'm right and you're wrong, which is the usual state of affairs around here. Why not bow to the inevitable and save us all a lot of trouble, Malcolm?''

''And the inevitable is…?'' Damn, he was folding.

Her smile said she knew it. ''Isn't it obvious? Tomorrow you hop in your little car and drive back to Santa Barbara and take another crack at it.''

''But—''

''That wasn't a request or a suggestion or anything of the sort,'' she informed him. ''It was an order. Do it.''

SABRINA OPENED the door herself. When she saw who it was, her smile slipped. ''You,'' she said.

Charley tried for a sincere smile and figured he got halfway. ''I hate to bother you again, but—''

''More papers to sign?'' she guessed, her voice sharp with suspicion.

''As a matter of fact…'' He lifted his briefcase up in front of him and snapped open the clasps.

Her dark expression cleared. ''Oh, okay. In that case, come on in.''

Charley couldn't believe she was for real. Did she actually believe he was here two days in a row on legitimate business? She really *was* rowing with one oar out of the water. But damn, her rowboat was gorgeous.

He followed her into the cool interior of the house,

which was really a mansion, but he wasn't thinking about that, too busy admiring the sway of her hips in brilliantly white shorts, the glorious sweep of long, lovely legs. Even her back and shoulders were delicate and graceful beneath pale-pink knit, emphasized by the swing of shimmering hair pulled up into a ponytail.

She led him through the house and out onto the terrace, where they'd shared drinks and dinner the previous evening. She indicated the table with one elegant arm.

"Please sit down. I'll ask Teresa to bring us something cold to drink."

He sat down, confused. She was acting as if nothing had happened. Okay, he could do that, too. He swung his briefcase onto the table and sat. By the time she returned with two tall glasses, he had the bogus papers spread before him.

She sat down and signed. She never read the papers, didn't ask any questions, just signed.

He frowned. "Aren't you curious as to what this is?" he asked, indicating the pages before them.

She looked surprised. "I know what they are," she assured him.

Somebody was seriously confused here. "You didn't ask and you didn't read. So tell me what you just signed."

Her smile sparkled; her teeth were as good as the rest of her, especially set off by luscious pink lips. "I just signed junk," she said serenely.

"*Junk!*" He recoiled, outraged before he could stop himself by realizing she'd seen right through him.

"Sure," she said. "Those papers were just an excuse to get you back in here again, right?"

"Right." He felt more than a little sheepish to have to admit it. "So why did you go along with it?"

"Because, dear Malcolm..." She leaned forward and patted his hand. "None of this is your fault. You're an innocent bystander. Why should I beat up on you for what my mother—what Lucretia's done and is still trying to do?"

"Some people would," he muttered.

"You're just the messenger," she said serenely. "Why should I chop off your head?"

At the moment, he felt as if she already had.

THIS TIME she gave him lunch while he tried to find an opening to make Lucretia's pitch. Even knowing Sabrina was waiting for it, probably even anticipating turning him down again, he found it hard to get started.

Teresa took away his empty plate and put a crystal dish of fresh fruit before him. Even depressed, he'd enjoyed her burritos and Spanish rice.

Sabrina indicated the fruit. "We grew all that," she said with obvious pride.

He looked at the contents of the dish more closely. "Even the bananas?"

"Yes. There are only a few areas in the United States where they'll grow. This is one of them."

"That's nice."

She peered at him more closely. "What's wrong, Malcolm?"

He sighed. "We've got to stop meeting this way."

That earned him a smile. "That's entirely up to

you. If you insist on allowing yourself to be used by
Lucretia as a pawn—''

"We've been through all that," he said, sounding
a bit testy even to himself.

"We've been through the other, too, but apparently
you've been sent to take us through it again."

"Yeah, apparently."

She leaned back in her chair, crossing her arms
beneath her breasts. "Then you may as well get it
over with."

He sucked in a deep breath. "You're right," he
agreed. "Okay, here it is. She categorically denies
she's trying to manipulate or control you. She merely
wants to give you the birthday party you deserve."

Her brows rose. "Deserve?"

"You know," he said. "As the heiress apparent."

She groaned. "Why can't Lucretia see…why can't
she accept the fact that I no longer want to be the
heiress apparent? I want to live a simple life, close to
the soil.…"

Charley had never heard such hogwash in his life.
Here she was, mistress of a fabulous multimillion-
dollar estate with servants at her beck and call, owner
of a ton of stock in a zillion-dollar company, and she
wanted a simple life? It was all he could do to keep
from laughing in her face.

His incredulity must have shown, for she stopped
talking in that dreamy voice and frowned at him.

"You don't believe me," she accused.

"Don't jump to conclusions."

"Oh. Then you *do* believe me."

"I said, don't jump to conclusions."

"Those are the only two options."

"No, there's a third." And he'd tell her what it was the minute he thought it up. "The third option is…" He floundered a bit, then went on with increasing confidence. "It doesn't matter whether I believe you or not. My opinion on your veracity isn't germane to what I'm here to do."

She frowned, wrinkling up that cute little nose. "But I *want* you to believe me, Malcolm."

"Sorry. It's not part of the job description."

"Neither is perpetuating the lies and deceit." She was breathing quickly, becoming perturbed.

"That's not what I'm doing," he objected. "Look, all your mother wants is for you to come to your birthday party. She's already issued invitations to most of the civilized world, for openers."

A delicate frown marred her smooth forehead. "She had no right to do that."

"You want to tell her what her rights are? I don't." He shuddered.

"I guess you couldn't," she admitted. "But, Malcolm, I can't let her get her hooks into me again. I can't. You don't know what it's like to have Lucretia Addison for a mother. She'll do anything—*any-thing*—to get her own way. She wants to tell me who my friends are, what to do with my time, how to spend my money and who to go out with."

"Sounds tough," he said with forked tongue. "I mean…" *Watch the sarcasm!* "To have someone love you so much she's willing to devote her entire life to your welfare, your happiness—"

"Welfare and happiness! That's not it at all." She pressed the back of one hand to her temple; for a moment she looked like a Victorian angel about to succumb to the vapors. "It's a power play, nothing more. I'd sooner die than lose what little ground I've gained in the past year."

"But—"

"I can't! Surely you can see that if I give her an inch, she'll take a mile."

"I—"

"I have to live my own life!"

Quick tears sprang artistically into her beautiful brown eyes. Charley found himself wondering how she did that, how she turned her head just right so that the tears sparkled like crystal chips.

Son of a bitch but she was gorgeous! And rich and spoiled and self-centered and—

Her emotion-drenched voice surrounded him. "You've got to go back and convince her to leave me alone, Malcolm."

"I couldn't do that, no way."

"But you'll try, won't you? For me...?"

Shit, he'd walk over fiery coals if she just kept looking at him like some tragic princess. He'd—

"I knew I could count on you, Malcolm."

The name broke into his lust-inspired coma. Charley bolted to his feet. "Sorry, Sabrina, but the answer's no." His voice came out a croak and he cleared his throat self-consciously. "I owe my loyalty to the woman who signs my paychecks."

"Really?" A surprised smile curved her luscious mouth and her big, brown eyes opened wide. "In that case, why don't you just quit that old job and come work for me? I'm sure I could find something for you to do...." She looked around as if she expected to find the perfect job for him just lying there on the ground.

Charley clenched his teeth to keep from snarling at her. And he thought her mother was insensitive! "Now you've gone and insulted me," he said, and it did sound a lot like a snarl.

She stared at him. "I'd never do such a thing. I meant every word I said. I'd love to have you on the payroll. I'm sure there's lots I could find for you to do, and you'd have the added benefit of a much healthier life-style. Fresh air—" She drew in a deep breath as if to show him how it was done. "Sunshine, healthy organic food, a generous vacation and pay package—"

She snapped her fingers as if with sudden inspiration. "I've got it! You could deal with Lucretia for me. That and handle all my Addison stock and other holdings. I had to fire my business manager because I found out he was in cahoots with my mother, but I could trust you. Couldn't I trust you?"

"No," he groaned. "Not only no but hell, no." Those big, brown eyes were driving him crazy, but not crazy enough to lie.

She didn't appear willing to accept that stark truth. "You're teasing me," she suggested with a tentative dimpled smile. "I *know* I could trust you."

"Not if I took advantage of your mental lapse, you couldn't. If I'd sell one boss down the tubes, *nobody* could trust me—hell, I couldn't trust myself. Besides, there's more involved than money."

"Such as?"

Such as a beautiful girl just begging to be taken

advantage of. "Sabrina," he said desperately, "this conversation is over."

Disgusted, he rose to his feet and picked up his jacket, once more discarded...and the tie along with it this time. If he kept trekking up here he'd soon be stripped down to his—

"Malcolm," she said sweetly, "you're a very moral man. My mother is lucky to have you, whether she knows it or not."

"Lucky? Yeah, sure. Now, about the birthday party—"

"Just tell her I said no."

"She won't like it."

"You can also tell her that I don't like her sending you up and down the coast to do her dirty work."

He leaped on that. "If she came herself—"

"I'd run," Sabrina said quickly. She gave a rueful little laugh, somehow looking incredibly vulnerable. "I'm much braver when I'm dealing with her long distance. When I'm with her she just..." She shivered. "She just overwhelms me. Does that make sense?"

More than she knew. "It's not necessary that your feelings make sense to *me,*" he said resolutely. "As you said yourself, I'm just the messenger."

Dimples twinkled in the creamy, smooth cheeks. "I think I like you, Malcolm."

Malcolm. "Sabrina," he said slowly. "I can honestly say that you don't know me well enough to have an opinion."

He flipped her a salute with his right hand and was gone.

"WELL?" Lucretia demanded. "How'd it go this time? Are you making progress, Malcolm?"

"No, I'm not." Charley slammed his briefcase on his desk and glared at it, then at her.

"That's not what I want to hear!" She began to pace in front of his desk. The carpet was only a year old and she'd already worn a path in it.

"Okay," he said, feeling disagreeable. "I'll lie to you—I'm making great progress. This time she gave me lunch along with innumerable, well-modulated but firm no's."

"Smart ass."

"I'm tired. There's a lot of tension involved in trying to lead a lamb to slaughter."

"Malcolm!" She stared at him with apparent horror.

He didn't feel even a twinge of guilt. "Hey, you *are* trying to manipulate the poor kid."

"How dare you suggest such a thing!"

"You want her married to a man of your choosing and this birthday party is nothing but a setup." How come his sympathies always lay with the absent Addison? When he was with Sabrina, he saw Lucretia's side of it; now with Lucretia his feelings were reversed.

He'd have to give that some thought.

"Well, really," she said. "And all this time I thought you understood—"

"I *understood* this job was dangerous when I took it. I just didn't know how dangerous."

She relaxed, a visible uncoiling of tension as if she'd just figured him out. "Malcolm, you can be quite a droll young man when the sprit moves you. Tell me the truth—she's weakening.''

"She's not weakening."

"Yes, she is. She gave you lunch."

"Last night she gave me dinner. She's not weakening. She just has excellent manners."

Lucretia's smile sparkled with pride. "She does, doesn't she? She learned everything she knows at her mother's knee."

Charley groaned. In that case, it was a wonder Sabrina didn't keep alligators in the swimming pool for the disposal of her mother's emissaries.

"She's weakening," Lucretia repeated.

"You're wrong." Something so obvious hardly seemed worth arguing about.

"She's weakening because she likes you."

"Now, there's a stretch."

"No, really. She talks to you—I can tell." She peered at him. "She does talk to you, doesn't she?"

"Well, yeah, sure." He shook his head impatiently. "I've learned more than I ever wanted to know about farming."

"Aha!"

"Aha what?"

"Aha, that farming operation is very important to her and she wouldn't tell you about it if she didn't like you. I was right to send you. You're worming your way into her confidence. I see it happening."

Charley shook his head. "She's polite, nothing more. She won't go to the party even if you've already invited Princess Di. Face it, Sabrina isn't interested, end of story."

He was looking at her, straight into her eyes, and

so he saw her flinch, saw the quick shadow of doubt…and maybe fear. She didn't want to believe him, but she *needed* to. He suddenly realized that Lucretia could be very, very hurt if she persisted in self-deception.

"Look, Lucy," he said as gently as he could manage, "you're setting yourself up for a fall."

"I don't agree—but what if I am?" Her chin came up, reminding him of her daughter. "A mother will risk anything for her child."

"But *your* child's a spoiled brat. She doesn't give a damn—"

"Don't talk about my daughter that way!"

Where Lucretia hadn't risen to her own defense, now she rose quickly to her daughter's. Her eyes flashed blue fire and she trembled with the force of her outrage.

"You're right," he said, sorry he'd hurt her by shooting off his mouth. "That was out of line. I apologize. Can we just go on to something else and chalk this up to—"

"No! Let me think—"

Sitting in the padded leather chair, he leaned back, waiting for her to come to her senses as she paced around, stopping, starting, flinging her arms about. This was the way she always thought. Lucretia Addison was a very physical woman; she liked to touch the objects in the room, wring her hands, rise on her toes like a prizefighter—and come to her own conclusions, as she did now. She stopped short before his desk, planted her fists on the blotter and leaned forward until she was right in his face.

"Here's what we're going to do," she announced.

"You're going back up there one more time, and you're going to tell her that—"

"The hell I am!" He stared at her. "This is no good."

"It *is* good. It's working. She's going to give in. Trust me."

He was shaking his head. "Enough's enough. Gimme a break here, okay?"

"Not a chance. You started it, you'll finish it."

"Or what?"

She pulled back, apparently blasted out of her self-absorption. "You'll finish it...or you're finished period. Do you get my drift, dear Malcolm?"

Well, hell, there it was, as bald as a billiard ball. Either Malcolm delivered Sabrina or he was finished at Addison Enterprises. So near to barbecue glory, yet so far.... He might as well start gathering up his belongings.

She spoke with all the guile she was capable of—which was a helluva lot of guile. "Don't give up now, Malcolm. We're on the verge of winning. You deliver Sabrina to her birthday party and I'll double the bonus check I mentioned when we agreed—"

"*We* agreed? You agreed!"

"Whatever. I'm prepared to put my money where my mouth is. Do this for me, Malcolm. Do this and earn my undying gratitude...and I can be very, very grateful."

Yeah, and so could a snake. How'd the story go about the little boy who put the snake in his pocket and then expressed surprise at being bitten? The snake had said, "You knew what I was when you picked me up."

And Charley knew what Lucretia Addison was when he signed on to work for her. She'd kept her part of their bargain; he'd learned more about big business than he'd realized there was to know. Not only that, but she'd paid him well, coming through with regular raises and even an occasional bonus.

But that wasn't why he hesitated now. No, it was her vulnerability, a vulnerability her daughter carried like a shield but that he'd never before seen in the mother.

That's what she was, first and foremost: a mother. A mother from hell, maybe, but a mother who loved her child, not wisely perhaps but too well.

At that point, Charley got mad, mad as hell. Not only was he about to lose the job that should have bought his dream, he was about to lose it over some spoiled princess living in La-La Land.

He wasn't about to go down without a fight.

"Okay," he said to Lucretia, "I'll do it. I'll take one more crack at getting the little princess to her own birthday party. But that's it—one more, do you get me? I don't think it'll work, but—"

"There's no place at Addison Enterprises for a quitter, Malcolm! Now go, and remember what's at stake here."

As if he could forget. "My job, my bonus," he muttered, picking up his briefcase.

"What's at stake here is a mother's love for her child, and what could be that child's last chance for happiness. Oh, Malcolm!" She threw herself at his chest and gave him a surprisingly strong hug. "Thank you! You'll never regret this, I swear."

Hell, he already regretted it.

5

"MY GOODNESS, Malcolm, you're back already?" Sabrina stared at him in astonishment, only belatedly remembering to invite him inside.

Grim-faced and stiff, he stomped through the doorway. She closed the door and turned to him with quick concern. This was not the cool, calm and collected Malcolm she knew.

"What is it?" she asked around a sudden shaft of alarm. "Has something happened to Lu—my mother?"

"Aha!" He glowered at her. "Now that you think something might have happened to her, all of a sudden she's not Lucretia—she's your *mother*."

"Why should that upset you so much?" Sabrina frowned, trying to understand his combative stance. "She's both, as you very well know. May I assume from your response that she *is* all right?"

"If you can call someone all right when her only child spits in her eye, not once but twice. Three strikes and we're all out, Sabrina."

That triggered a smile. "You're not out, Malcolm. Lucretia is. Don't take it so personally! As you pointed out yourself, you're just the messenger."

He sighed, his face a study in frustration. Poor Malcolm! It must be tough to work for Lucretia, Sabrina thought. It certainly was tough to be her daughter.

She pasted a tolerant expression on her face and laced her fingers together at her waist. "All right, say what you've come to say—again."

"Okay." He squared his shoulders. "Your mother wants to give you a birthday party. For some reason, she thinks it'll be better if you're there. She's inviting you to attend. She's begging you to attend. *I'm* begging you to attend."

"No, thank you."

He stared at her. "That's really cold," he said at last.

At his implied criticism, she felt heat rush into her cheeks. "You don't know. You just don't know, Malcolm." She raised one hand to fist above her heart. "All my life I've had to fight for my independence. She's lied to me, misled me—manipulated and tricked me—"

"Maybe she's changed," he suggested hopefully.

"And maybe the moon is made of green cheese. No." She shook her head for emphasis. "She is what she is."

"You don't believe people can change?"

"Some of them, maybe. Not Lucretia."

"How about you?"

"If I wanted to." She wondered where was he headed with this. The truth was, she had no desire to change. She was right and Lucretia was wrong. No change was called for on Sabrina's side of the issue.

He put his hands on her shoulders and stared into her eyes. "Then change your mind and come to your birthday party."

He'd never deliberately touched her before and the strength of his grip surprised and somehow pleased her. She liked strong people; they made her feel safe. All except her mother, of course. She refocused on the subject at hand. "I can't."

"You said you were capable of change."

"No, I said…" She let her words trail off and uttered a tragic sigh. "You don't know what I've been through, Malcolm. You have no idea—"

"Don't I?" His fingers spasmed, digging into her shoulders.

"Nobody does." It didn't even occur to her to pull away. "No one would believe what she's put me through, even if I told them."

"What have you put *her* through?"

"Why, nothing!"

"Com' on. I hear that most kids put their parents through plenty."

"Not me," Sabrina insisted, blinking back self-righteous tears. She knew he'd understand her decision; people always saw things her way. "Honesty is the most important thing in the world to me," she said fervently. "I can't abide lying and never do it myself. Yet Lucretia—"

"Bull," Malcolm said. Releasing her, he stepped away, thrusting his hands behind his back as if to keep himself from grabbing her again…or something.

Sabrina blinked in astonishment. "I beg your pardon?"

"Nobody's perfect, Sabrina."

"Of course not." But some were close; she knew that for a fact.

"You're really that hot for the truth, are you?"

A warning tingle traveled down her spine. "Of course."

He indicated the two of them. "You mean from me, too, or do your high standards just apply to your mother?"

"Malcolm, you're confusing me." Turning away, she started through the house toward the decks and terraces in back. "Why don't we get a nice cool drink and—"

He dogged her heels. "Don't you want to hear what I think about all this?"

She stopped so suddenly that he stepped on her heels and had to put his hands on her arms again to help her keep her balance. "Is that all?" She turned to him with a dimpled smile. "Of course I'm interested in your thoughts, Malcolm. Perhaps you know a way I can keep her from *doing* this to me all the time? Do you think—"

"I think," he cut in, his gaze holding hers, "that you're a spoiled brat, Sabrina Addison."

For a moment she stood there stunned, feeling as if he'd socked her in the stomach with his fist. By the time she caught her breath, she'd also figured out what was going on. She smiled at him with relief. "You're teasing me," she suggested confidently. "I can take a joke, fortunately." She added brightly, "Would you like iced tea or lemonade? A snack?"

"I'm not joking."

The tone of his voice left no room for misunderstanding. This time when she turned, it was slowly and in disbelief. "You're...not kidding!"

"I'm not kidding, I'm not joking, I'm not having a good time here."

"Then..." She frowned, seeking to understand. "You really think I'm a spoiled brat?" Nobody had ever suggested such a thing. *Nobody!* Therefore it couldn't possibly be true.

Could it?

"I'm not suggesting it," Malcolm announced grimly. "I'm saying it straight out." He raked both hands through his smooth hair and it fell back into perfect place. "You're spoiled, also ungrateful and self-centered. I'm sorry, but it's true."

Her mouth fell open. "Malcolm!"

"I'm sorry, but it's true." He didn't look sorry; he looked mad as hell. "You claim to value the truth above all else."

"I do! But..." She chewed on her lower lip, uncertain how to proceed. This was an absolute and totally new experience to her. No one had ever talked to her this way.

Malcolm's lip curled, derisively, she thought.

"Would it hurt you to go to your own birthday party?" he demanded. "All that woman wants to do is make you happy! She's the same woman who's made you richer than God by giving you a zillion dollars' worth of stock in her company. She's also showered you with everything your little heart desires, including this mansion where you can play landed gentry. And what does she ask in return? For you to go to your own f-f-flaming birthday party!"

"If you'd try to see my side of it—"

"Your side! Your side? Too many people have seen your side. It's time someone tried to see *her* side!"

"You must really like her a lot to say that," she

suggested, unable to digest the increasingly obvious fact that he was actually taking her mother's side against her.

"I—" He stopped cold and his face took on a stricken expression.

She saw his weakness and exploited it mercilessly. "The truth, Malcolm...remember?"

"Well, hell." He looked as if he'd just been caught in his own trap. "You can *never* repeat this."

"Moi?" She pressed an innocent hand to her innocent breast and cultivated an innocent expression.

"Okay," he said grimly, "I guess I have gone too far to stop now. So as a matter of fact, your mother drives me crazy most of the time."

"Then why don't you quit?" she asked—an entirely appropriate question if what he said was true.

"Because in spite of everything, I *like* her. Don't ask me why, because I don't have a clue." He began to pace, waving his arms. "On top of that, she pays good—real good. Some of us aren't independently wealthy and therefore find such details important."

She felt a defensive flush rise into her cheeks. "That's a cheap shot. I've never asked her for a thing."

"But you sure were willing to take everything she offered, as long as it benefited *you*." He waved aside her protests. "Don't stop me now—I'm on a roll. In the second place, I don't quit because the woman's practically a genius."

Now she knew he'd lost it. "Don't be ridiculous. She didn't even go to college."

He stared at her. "You're kidding."

"I'm not. She inherited the business."

"In that case, she really *is* a genius, because she can put together a business deal better than anyone I've ever seen or heard tell of. I've learned a lot from your mother, Sabrina Addison."

She shivered. "I can see that. You've certainly learned not to pull your punches."

"Hey, you asked for the truth." He was fairly glowering. "In the third place, I saw her reaction when you turned her down the first time and the second time. There's not much that *can* hurt her, but you did it. Family takes precedence over everything else with her. She thinks you walk on water."

Sabrina gave a dismissive sniff. "I'd laugh if I didn't feel more like crying. She thinks I'm her...her chattel, to be bossed around and manipulated and brought out for the amusement of her guests."

"She loves you."

"I love her." Tears welled in Sabrina's eyes. "But her kind of love...smothers me."

"Yeah, right. And after all these years you haven't figured out a way to handle her." He rolled his eyes, indicating disbelief. "Okay, in the fourth place—" He stopped talking and walking and clamped his teeth together hard.

"In the fourth place, what?" she urged, figuring she might as well hear it all.

"I got carried away. There is no fourth place." He turned, halted, turned back. "Or maybe there is."

He stepped up right in front of her and stared into her eyes. "You're a selfish little rich girl who's living in a dreamworld. If you'd try just a little, you could see your mother's side of this. But you won't make even that much effort. You treat everybody around you like stage props, and you slip from your 'lady of the manor' mode to your 'tragic princess' persona without missing a beat.''

He paused for breath. She met his gaze, crushed at such a blanket condemnation.

"You don't *really* believe all that," she said at last, trying to cajole him out of his bad mood. Goodness, what had set him off? He had nothing personal to lose in all this.

"I *do* believe it." His voice rang with conviction. "I will now go back and tell your mother that I not only failed in my assignment, but that I managed to completely alienate her little darling for all time."

Alienated? Sabrina watched him go as if through a mist, thinking, he thought he'd *alienated* her? Hardly! She wasn't alienated at all by the totally unexpected things he'd said. He was perhaps the first person she'd ever met who was willing to talk straight to her. She wasn't alienated; she was *enchanted.*

CHARLEY DROVE back to the city.

Three times he'd tried and three times he'd failed to complete his mission. The fact that he was dealing with a gorgeous female who drove him wild on a number of levels would cut no ice with Lucretia Addison.

Maybe he *should* have hit Sabrina with his *real* fourth point: that if she didn't come around he'd not only lose the bonus he so desperately needed, but in all likelihood he'd lose his job, as well.

Nah. He could never have said that. It sounded too much like whining.

Lucretia was waiting for him, naturally. This time

she whisked him into her own office before letting out her breath on a long note of frustration. "Well?" she demanded. "Tell me what happened."

"What happened." Suddenly very tired, Charley helped himself to a seat. "She said no. She's made of ice. Nothing I said moved her in the slightest."

Lucretia caught her breath. "Did you tell her how much this means to me?"

"Yes."

"Did you tell her I had no ulterior motives?"

"Yes."

"Did you tell her I love her?"

He hated to do this to her. "Yes. Nothing worked. She's unshakable."

She threw up her hands, frustration emanating from her like a heat shield. "And that's all? You tucked your tail between your legs and slunk away?"

"I don't slink."

Her brows rose. "Well, excuse me! It's just a figure of speech, Malcolm. So what did you say to upset her?"

"What makes you think I—"

"Because she said *no,* and I'm sure she wanted to say yes. Somehow you blew it. Tell me." She gestured with the fingers of one hand.

The jig, Charley realized, was well and truly up this time. Might as well go down with guns blazing. "I told her she was a spoiled brat. I told her a bit more after that, but I think that was what did it for her."

"You...called...my...daughter...a...*brat* to her face?"

"Hey," Charley said modestly, "she wanted the truth. I calls 'em like I sees 'em."

"So do I," she agreed, grim faced. "You're fired."

He stood up, almost relieved to have it over with. "I thought you might see it that way," he said, suddenly calm.

His reaction obviously confused Lucretia. "You might be able to change my mind if you came up with something I could use to get her to come around," she wheedled. "Did she give you a clue why she was taking this tack? Do you think she—"

"No, I don't." Charlie shook his head—he hoped decisively. "Look, I don't work for you any longer, so I'm outta here."

She looked completely taken aback. "But you don't have enough money yet for that restaurant you're so obsessed with," she argued. "You may still escape the ax if you'll work with me here."

The hair at his nape stood on end. "What do you know about a restaurant?" he challenged.

She looked startled by his vehemence. "Nothing. Nothing at all. It's just that all young men want *something* like that. Sabrina—"

But he was walking away, ignoring her. She called after him.

"I've fired you before and taken you back, but don't think that will happen this time! If you walk out of that door without giving me some ray of hope that Sabrina will come around—"

"You can't fire me," he called over his shoulder. "I quit!"

He walked out of Addison Enterprises a free man.

Hell, maybe he could get a job in somebody else's barbecue restaurant.

SABRINA WAS WAITING for Lucretia's telephone call and it came in right on schedule.

"How are you, dear?"

"Fine, Lucretia. What can I do for you?"

"You could say you'll come to your birthday party but that might be asking too much."

"Don't be coy. It doesn't become you."

"What's become of your sense of humor? I was only joking."

"Oh."

Lucretia's groan came clearly over the wire. "Don't be mad at me, sweetie. I know that idiot Malcolm upset you, but don't take it out on dear old Mom."

"He upset me, all right."

She'd thought of little else since he'd left. She'd almost hoped Lucretia would send him back up the coast again, but realized *four* tries with the same messenger would be a bit much even for her mother. Three had been stretching it, actually.

"I made sure he paid for his impudence," Lucretia assured her. "No employee of Addison Enterprises can go around insulting *my* daughter with impunity."

Sabrina's antennae, always on alert where her mother was concerned, pricked up even more. "What do you mean, he paid for it?"

"I fired him. What else? And forget that bonus—"

"What bonus?"

"He didn't tell you? I promised him a bonus if he

could get you to see reason. I mean, fair is fair. You scratch my back and I'll scratch—"

"He didn't tell me." So that had been his fourth point; he was poor and needed that bonus, maybe to buy food or pay his rent. Maybe he even supported an aged grandmother or was putting a younger sibling through school. Sabrina's heart fluttered. What a man!

He hadn't wanted to influence her that way. He was obviously an honest, upright human being, not part of the human sludge too often surrounding her mother.

Lucretia spoke then, with complete insensitivity. "Why should he tell you? It didn't matter to anyone in the world except him and he's blown it big-time. He—"

"But you fired him? You fired Malcolm because of *me?*"

"Well, certainly." Lucretia sounded baffled by the question. "Sabrina, I would fire every employee I've got if it would make you happy. But seriously, how could I work with the man, day after day, knowing he'd insulted my only child? *Maybe* I could overlook his failure to complete a simple task efficiently, but—"

"Hire him back!"

"Sabrina, what on earth are you shouting about?"

"Hire him back at once! I mean it, Mother!"

"Mother. You called me 'Mother.'"

"It was a slip of the tongue." Sabrina tried to rein in her indignation. "Will you give him back his job or not?"

"Well, I...that is, I don't know...he *did* insult you, dear."

"He didn't mean any of that stuff. Or at least, not

much of it.'' She suspected he had meant the part about Lucretia driving him crazy, but wild horses wouldn't drag that out of her. She struggled to put her thoughts into words. "He made me feel like a real person for a change, not like a...a pretty picture on somebody's wall."

"Darling! Has someone been mean to you?"

Lucretia would never understand, even if she lived to be a hundred. "Will you give him back his job or not?"

"I...guess I could. I mean, I'd like to—he was the best assistant I ever had and I'd pegged him for great things. But under the present circumstances, I'll probably have to humiliate myself to get him to come back." She paused, calculating. "And if I do?"

Sabrina groaned. Lucretia always kept her eye on the main chance. "All right," she said, "I catch your drift. Yes, I'll go to that, that stupid birthday party if you—"

"I knew you would. Oh, darling, you won't be sorry! Twenty-five is such a wonderful age. You're going to love the plans I've—"

"Hold on!" This was no time to soften, Sabrina warned herself sternly. "I'll go on one condition—make that two conditions."

"Anything. Name it."

"You've got to get Malcolm back to work."

"Done. No problem. I'll take care of that. This is going to be marvellous. Why don't I just—"

"Lucretia! I said two conditions. Here's the other one...."

CHARLEY SPENT a miserable night going over and over his bank book and trying to figure out how to earn the rest of the money he needed. There was no obvious way.

Brooding over his morning coffee and wishing he'd never heard the name Addison, he was roused by a pounding on his apartment door.

Lucretia stood there—basic blue from head to foot, dripping pearls. She looked bright eyed and eager and, as always, in command. "Well?" she challenged him. "Aren't you going to invite me in?"

"No!" He shut his mouth and started to slam the door, when he saw the long, pointed toe of one hand-made Italian shoe blocking the threshold and thought better of it. "What do you want?" he demanded gruffly. "Blood?"

"Droll," she said, brushing him aside with the sweep of one arm and marching inside. In the middle of his efficiency unit, she paused and looked around curiously. "You *live* here?"

"Oh, no," he said ingenuously. "I live in Beverly Hills. This is just my town closet."

She patted his unshaven cheek with one manicured hand. "Did I offend you, dear boy? So sorry. Your...pied-à-terre caught me by surprise."

"Your...*visit* caught me by surprise. Now, why don't you run along and pull the wings off a butterfly or something?"

"Malcolm!" She summoned up that hurt expression he knew so well but hardly ever fell for anymore. "Is that any way to greet your boss?" She sniffed the air like a lioness seeking meat. "Is that coffee I smell? I'll have a cup, thank you very much."

She sat down at his plastic-topped dinette set and plunked her expensively tooled leather briefcase on the floor by her feet. Folding her hands on the table, she waited.

He poured her coffee and warmed his own. "Okay, you want to tell me?"

"All in good time. First I want you to know that the Hong Kong merger is moving ahead without a snag, thanks to you."

"I didn't do much."

"Don't be modest. It doesn't become you. Also, I received a call from Edward Edwards while you were gone yesterday and he said that because of your quick action he'd been able to..."

She rattled on and Charley let her, mostly because he couldn't stop her. Slowly it dawned on him just how nervous she was. She had a burr under her saddle, no doubt about it.

Then it further dawned on him that she was trying to apologize to him without actually admitting that she'd screwed up when she'd fired him. But *why* had she seen the light, and so quickly at that? It sure as hell wasn't because of Hong Kong or Edward Edwards.

Sabrina.

It had to be Sabrina, but why would she rise to his defense after what he'd said to her? Once he'd cooled down, he'd been ashamed of that. Everything he'd said was true, of course, but he didn't remember that so much as the wounded expression on her beautiful face, those Bambi-brown eyes looking at him while tears, sparkling like diamonds, spilled down her cheeks.

"Malcolm! Pay attention here."

"Sorry." He blinked back to the present, frowning.

"You wanna quit wasting both our time and tell me what the hell you're doing here?"

She recoiled in her plastic-padded chair. "I should think it would be obvious."

"Trust me, it's not."

"You're joking, of course. I don't suppose I can blame you, actually. A man's feelings can be so easily hurt."

"Yes, that often happens to me when I'm called an idiot and fired all in the same breath."

Lucretia's broad smile quivered only slightly around the edges. "Exactly! But now that the smoke has cleared, I'm ready to be big about it and let bygones be bygones. I've decided to give you another chance, Malcolm. You can come back to work."

"You're ready to *be* what and *do* what? You didn't fire me, Lucy. I quit." He felt his blood rising all over again at the memory.

"A technicality." She waved it aside. "Now will you get dressed? George is waiting downstairs."

George was Lucretia's chauffeur. She called all her chauffeurs "George."

He looked down at his wrinkled seersucker bathrobe and was glad he'd bothered to put it on after rolling out of bed this morning. Otherwise, Lucretia might have had a nasty shock. The thought made him grin.

"See," she said triumphantly. "You're smiling. You know I'm right."

"I never said—"

"Ten percent raise."

His ears pricked up. "Ten percent?"

"Oh, all right. You drive a hard bargain. Fifteen percent, but not a penny more."

She said all that in a jovial manner, as if they were simply playing a mutually agreed-upon game. In that moment, Charley realized that *both* the Addison women were certifiably nuts.

But money talked, at least to a lad from the wrong side of Kansas City. "Done." He stood up.

She stopped him with a hand on his wrist. "Uh, just one more little thing, Malcolm dear."

He froze; this was where she told him she'd just been yanking his chain and fired him all over again.

She licked her lips. "I spoke to Sabrina."

"I figured." She kept her grip on him, but he remained standing.

"Sabrina has agreed to go to her birthday party."

"She's *what?*" Now he did sit down, with a bang. Lucretia nodded. "That is, she's agreed...with strings."

"Which are?"

"She wants *you* there."

"Me?" Now she had his attention. "Why? So she can play pin the tail on the ass—"

"I wondered myself," Lucretia cut in, "but I think I've figured it out."

"Care to share?"

"She expects she'll be surrounded by my friends and business associates—"

"Sycophants."

"Whatever. I suspect she figures she'll need at least one person around who will talk straight to her."

"That's the dumbest—" He stopped himself, remembering what happened when you insulted the princess.

She darted him a dagger-sharp glance. "We'll give her what she wants. You'll come along, listen to what she has to say and report back to me."

"In other words," Charley interpreted, "spy."

"'Spy' is such a nasty word." She brushed at a speck of imaginary dust on her sleeve.

"That's what you want, though."

"Of course, but it's still a nasty word. What do you say, Malcolm? And remember—the bonus rule is back into effect."

He was about to bolt, breathing fire, when to his astonishment, Lucretia rose up and kissed his cheek. "Rush, dear boy. We've got a lot to do today."

It was probably as close as she'd ever come to expressing sincere gratitude.

6

Before he got into the mile-long limo, Malcolm told Lucretia in no uncertain terms that he wasn't going to spy for her. He told her again on the way to the office and several more times over the course of the day.

He thought she understood, but with Lucretia it was impossible to be sure.

By the end of the day, he harbored a reasonable hope that his work life was back to normal. She was a demanding boss, but he didn't mind that, so long as she kept her distance and let him keep his. He'd begun to hope that actually might happen, right up to seven-thirty, when he began to clear off his desk at the end of the long workday.

Lucretia stuck her head into his office. "You're leaving already?"

"Already," he said calmly.

"Okay." She sounded grudging. "I'd hoped you'd be able to work up that schedule I spoke to you about—"

The light, mellifluous voice of the one and only Sabrina Addison wafted from the next room. "Lucretia, you're a slave driver."

Startled down to his socks, Charley swung around and saw her standing there, looking gorgeous.

She was a vision dressed all in pastel blue—his favorite color—with her long hair tumbling in curls from the top of her head and diamonds sparkling on her earlobes and around her wrist and throat. The skirt ended several inches above her knees, drawing attention to long, sleek legs and slender feet in matching blue slippers.

"Darling!" Lucretia rushed to embrace her recalcitrant child.

Over her mother's shoulder, Sabrina met Charlie's gaze and winked, as if they shared some delicious secret.

He, on the other hand, didn't have a clue what the woman was up to now. He waited, maintaining his stoic expression with some difficulty. Then again, when he was around the princess, everything seemed difficult.

Lucretia pulled back to smile proudly on her offspring. "What brings you to the city, my darling? Why didn't you call? I could have planned something special. As it is, I've got one of those awful business dinners planned with the president of—oh, what the hell! I'll cancel. Malcolm, call—"

"Hey, slow down." Laughing, Sabrina removed herself from Lucretia's grip. "You don't need to do that. I didn't come in to see you— I mean," she amended hastily, apparently seeing Lucretia's disappointment, "not entirely."

"Then what?" Lucretia still looked disgruntled.

Sabrina cocked her head and smiled at Charley. "I came to see Malcolm—I mean, to see if he was back at work and everything was on an even keel again."

"I told you it was." Lucretia looked offended.

"I know you did," Sabrina agreed cheerfully, "but I wanted to see for myself."

Charley acknowledged her concern with a dip of his head. "As you can see, everything is hunky-dory. Your interest is gratefully acknowledged, but unnecessary."

"That's good." Sabrina walked to his desk. "I felt responsible for your troubles, actually. You didn't tell me that you had a personal stake in all this... nonsense."

"Because it had no place in your decision," he said, remaining cool and distant.

She smiled that dazzling smile. "Are you saying a woman's gotta do what a woman's gotta do?"

"That would be my guess." Charley stood up. "If you ladies will excuse me, I'll—"

"Of course," Lucretia said.

"No, wait!" Sabrina countered. She turned to her mother. "I feel I owe Malcolm some consideration for giving him such a hard time, so I'm going to—"

"Not at all," Charley interrupted. The last thing he wanted from Sabrina Addison was consideration.

Lucretia slipped an arm around Sabrina's shoulders. "He's right, dear. You don't owe him anything. Let me cancel my business dinner and take you out somewhere elegant."

"No, thank you." Sabrina removed her mother's arm adroitly. "I came to take *Malcolm* to dinner—to make amends. You understand, of course."

"Oh, no!" Charley and Lucretia said in tandem, he with horror and she with who knows what.

"Oh, yes," Sabrina said serenely. She slipped one small hand through the crook of his arm and smiled up at him. "This time *I* need to talk to *you*. When you came to me, I listened—several times. How can you possibly do less?"

How, indeed? She had a way of twisting his own actions and words around to suit herself, but since she always did it with a smile, he couldn't find it in him to protest too vigorously.

SHE INSISTED that he choose a place *he'd* like to go, and he, in a stubborn fit, did just that. Porky's was not exactly Sabrina Addison's kind of place, but what the hell? Charley had been aching to sample what was heralded as Kansas City barbecue ever since the place opened a couple of weeks ago, but a killer work schedule had kept him away.

He'd expected Sabrina to seem at least a little out of her element, but she didn't. She didn't look down on the place; she looked around on it, seeming delighted with every funky detail.

Porky's had taken over space vacated by a taco joint, and nobody had bothered to remove the dusty serapes and sombreros that provided "atmosphere." Diners sat at old wooden picnic tables with metal holders for paper napkins and bottles of ketchup.

Sabrina took the seat Charley indicated, smiling at him. "This place is cute," she announced.

"'Cute'?" He took off his suit coat, unknotted his tie, then slipped that off, too.

"It also smells good." She sniffed appreciatively of the aromas wafting from the kitchen. "Do you come here often?"

"First time." Charley unbuttoned his collar and sat down on a wooden bench. Reaching for a plastic-backed menu, he flipped it open. Taking one quick look, he groaned.

"What is it?" Sabrina leaned forward, looking interested.

"I think we've stumbled onto a hoax here."

"Excuse me?" Her lovely face looked puzzled.

"If this is Kansas City barbecue, I'm a monkey's uncle."

She laughed. "How do you know? You haven't tasted it yet."

"I don't have to, although I'm willing to take a shot at it." He jerked his chin toward the menu on the table between them. "My guess is we're talking Memphis here."

"As in Tennessee?"

"Yeah. They'll barbecue anything in Memphis—hell, they'll barbecue baloney."

She laughed, apparently with delight. "That doesn't sound too bad."

"Get outta here!" But he gave her a reluctant smile. "They'll also cook it over *anything,* including charcoal and gas."

She propped her elbows on the table and rested her chin in cupped hands. She then proceeded to look at him as if he was the most interesting man in the whole wide world. "Charcoal and gas are bad?"

"Let's just say that for barbecue, wood's better." Jeez, he sounded pompous, even to himself. "I like hickory and oak myself. Of course, in Texas they also use a lot of mesquite, which is a noxious—"

"What'll it be, man?" A large man wearing a mostly white apron held his order pad at the ready.

"Are you Porky?" Charley asked.

"Nah, I'm lean as a greyhound." The waiter laughed uproariously. "Sorry, man, I couldn't resist. Porky ain't here. What can I get you folks?" He included an appreciative grin at Sabrina, who gave him a sparkling smile.

"Malcolm will order for me," she said confidently.

"Malcolm!" The waiter guffawed in Charley's direction. "And you're makin' jokes about Porky?"

Charley decided not to get into it. "Bring me ribs, and the lady will have pork shoulder, chopped." He glanced at her for guidance. "Want a beer?" He'd never met a woman in his life less likely to want a beer.

"I'd love a beer," she said.

The waiter ran through the available brands and they made their selections. Then he added, "We got baked beans, coleslaw, potato salad, French fries and spaghetti. You get your choice of two, so what'll it be?"

"Spaghetti?" Sabrina looked incredulous.

Charley grimaced at the waiter. "With barbecue sauce on it, right?"

"You got it, man."

"Memphis," Charley said darkly.

Sabrina gave the waiter a friendly smile. "It sounds good to me," she announced. "I'll have spaghetti and...and...no green salad?"

"That's for sissies. We got coleslaw and potato."

Sabrina swallowed hard. "Coleslaw," she said gamely.

Charley ordered beans and coleslaw and the waiter tromped away, to return minutes later with the beer.

Sabrina sipped hers as daintily as if it were wine, looking relaxed and happy to be there.

Which didn't make a helluva lot of sense to Charley, but who was he to argue with the boss's daughter?

Setting her bottle on the table, she licked her lips prettily. He braced himself for whatever might come next.

"I'm sorry about everything that happened," she said suddenly.

He blinked. "Everything?"

She shrugged. "All those trips you made to Santa Barbara. And then getting fired after you'd done your best. Really, Lucretia is too much!"

"Yeah, she can be." He watched her warily, wondering where this was leading.

"I couldn't let her get away with it, not after what you did for me."

"What exactly did I do for you?" he wondered cautiously. "As I recall, I said some pretty harsh things to you on that last trip. I've regretted it ever since, if you want to know the truth."

"Oh, no!" Her beautiful brown eyes flew wide. "That was the part I liked best."

"The part where I called you a 'spoiled brat'? I don't think so."

She laughed somewhat ruefully. "That *was* a bit harsh. But yes, that's the part I mean—the part where you told me the truth as you saw it." She leaned forward, speaking earnestly. "I value the truth above all things, Malcolm. When I thought about what you'd said, I realized that I'd finally found someone I could trust."

"How do you figure that?" Charley was now definitely convinced that this babe was playing volleyball without a net.

"You're an honest man," she answered, looking surprised he'd ask.

"I am when I can afford to be," he hedged. Yeah, he was honest...but he'd been had a time or two in his twenty-nine years.

"You're being modest. I know I can trust you, and that's why I insisted you come to my birthday party."

"About that, Sabrina—"

"Chow's here!" The waiter plunked down platters heaped high with food, accompanied by a small pitcher of barbecue sauce. "You folks need anything else?"

Sabrina eyed her food doubtfully. "No, thank you. This looks just wonderful."

"Y'all eat up, then. Holler if you need anything." The waiter hustled away to take another order.

"I've never seen so much food in my life," Sabrina whispered in an awed tone.

"Quantity over quality," Charley predicted, examining with a practiced eye his own heaping pile of ribs. "Dry ribs."

"Dry?" She picked up her fork.

"Cooked with a dry rub, sauce to be added at the table." He picked up a rib. It looked all right: crisp and brown and fragrant. He took a tentative bite and found the meat fall-off-the-bone tender.

"Not bad," he admitted grudgingly. Reaching for the sauce, he poured a pool of it on the edge of his platter, dipped the rib and took another bite.

"Well?" Sabrina nudged. "How is it?"

"Not my cup of tea." Charley grimaced. "What the hell's in there...*butter?*"

"How'd you learn so much about barbecue?" Sabrina wondered aloud. She picked up a small bite of pork and tasted it, her expression showing her surprise. "Wow, that's really good." She reached for the pitcher of sauce.

Charley did not want to discuss his almost lifelong obsession with barbecue with this merely inquisitive female. It was too important to him and he'd already given too much away. Bad enough that Lucretia had an inkling.

So he just shrugged. "About me coming to your birthday party..."

She looked up with such a pleased expression that he felt like a jerk even bringing this up.

"Yes, Malcolm?"

"I wouldn't belong there. I'd just be in the way."

"Not at all."

She licked barbecue sauce off those luscious lips but a touch still smeared her chin. Without thinking, Charley reached across the table to blot it away with his own napkin. Their glances met and he found himself swallowing hard and yanking his hand away.

He tried again. "I still work for your mother. I'm an employee, not a friend."

"Can't you be both?"

"I...don't see how."

"Don't you want to be my friend, Malcolm?" She turned upon him an expression that would have brought tears to a statue, as if the only thing she needed to make her happy in this lifetime was his friendship.

"Well, sure, only—I guess I—you don't—" Charley stumbled to a halt. "Jeez, Sabrina!" He'd just have to tell her the truth to get her to back off. "Your mother wants me to go so I can spy on you for her."

"Of course." She tried the coleslaw and gasped. "What in the world is in this stuff?"

He frowned. "You know what she's up to?"

"The same thing she's always up to."

"And you still insist you want me along?"

"Oh, Malcolm." She gave him a melting smile. "I want you there because I can count on you. You won't spy for her."

"I won't spy for you, either," he warned.

"I don't expect you to."

"Then what the hell—"

"All I expect you to do is tell me the truth, just like you did before. If I'm being unreasonable, I want you to say so. If I'm acting like a spoiled brat—" She burst out laughing, then shook her head. "That one I just can't see, but if you do, I expect you to say so."

He stared at her incredulously. "You want me to be your conscience?"

She nodded with determination. "Will you do it? If you won't, I'm afraid I won't be able to go at all."

For a moment they sat there in a silence so intense that it fairly hummed. Then he sighed.

"Just call me 'Jiminy Cricket,'" he groused.

She placed her small hand over his large one, squeezing lightly. "I'd rather call you 'my friend,'" she said with a touching naïveté that made him want to...well, he told himself that he'd like to give her a good shaking and tell her to wake up, but that was a lie.

What he wanted to do to Sabrina Addison went way beyond shaking her.

AFTER THAT, life returned to normal, more or less. Lucretia still drove him crazy most of the time, but Charley was accustomed to that. He knew Sabrina's birthday party was approaching with the momentum of a steam locomotive, but he kept that knowledge tucked away in the back of his mind because he just didn't want to deal with it.

And then it was there, staring him in the face. On the morning in August, Lucretia picked him up in her limo and the two of them drove to meet Sabrina at Channel Islands Harbor, where Lucretia kept her yacht.

Charley rolled his eyes when he saw it. It looked bigger than a football field and had *sails*. "What the hell is that?" he muttered. "The *Queen Mary* with wings?"

Sabrina's silvery laughter sent shivers down his spine. She wore shorts and a T-shirt and sneakers, all so sparkling white they blinded him.

"It's a sixty-seven-foot cutter with a double spreader masthead rig and double headsail," she said cheerfully, as if she expected him to understand. "Nothing but the best for my—for Lucretia."

Lucretia gave her daughter a pained glance. "You can call me 'Mother,' darling. That's who I am."

"I could call you a lot of things," Sabrina responded coolly, "but good manners forbid."

"She's joking," Lucretia assured Charley.

He wasn't as sure about that as Lucretia seemed to be.

LUCRETIA HAD OBVIOUSLY planned a leisurely trip to Addison Island, arranging for dinner to be served on board the elegant vessel before they arrived at their destination. Sailing out of the harbor beneath the billowing sails, breathing the clear salt air, Charley felt as if he'd fallen through some rabbit hole and come out in another world.

The world of the rich and famous, he thought, sitting in an air-conditioned salon overlooking the whitecapped Pacific Ocean and looking out through wraparound windows. A steward served champagne and Lucretia raised her glass.

"To my daughter," she announced. "To her happiest birthday yet."

"I'll drink to that." Charley did.

"Oh, Lucretia!" Sabrina made a modest face.

Charley settled back in the glove-leather upholstery of the small settee. He'd never experienced such elegance in his life, hadn't even known such luxury existed outside a movie theater.

The room itself was a marvel. A recessed library dominated one side and built into other walls were a recessed wine and crystal cabinet beside a bar with stools, and an entertainment center with an enormous television. Soft music came from speakers hidden around the room. Beneath his feet lay a flat-woven natural-colored carpet that was understated, yet somehow rich.

Sabrina watched his silent perusal with a slight

smile playing around her lips. "Would you like the grand tour?" she offered lightly.

He hesitated, then decided what the hell. How many chances would he ever get to tour a yacht with a beautiful woman for his guide?

"Sure," he said, rising. "That is, if Lucy doesn't have something she'd like me to be doing?"

"Shoo!" Lucretia waved her hands at him. "You young people run along. Sabrina, I'll be in my office if you need me. Dinner's at six and we'll put in at the island about nine."

"We'll come running when we hear the dinner bell," Sabrina promised. She held out one hand to Charley, smiling. "Shall we go?"

He ignored the hand. "Lead the way," he said. "I'm right behind you."

She gave him a pained glance, then shrugged and turned away.

"WHY IS THIS BOAT named the *Lizzie J.?*" Charley asked. "That's a mundane name for such a fancy craft."

Leaning beside him against the rail, Sabrina gave him a lazy smile. "It's named for Lucretia, actually."

"Then why isn't it the *Lucretia A.?*" There, that sounded quite reasonable in spite of the six or eight glasses of champagne he'd had during the course of the tour.

"Because," Sabrina said, looking at him over her shoulder, "she picked the name Lucretia herself. Her real name is Lizzie Jean. She changed it, not that I blame her."

He shook his head. Nothing was what it seemed,

not even the names of the players. "You're really Sabrina, right?"

"Well..." She let it play out as if he'd made a joke.

Charley sighed and let his attention wander out to sea. The tour had left him practically tongue-tied. He'd never seen so much shiny teak in his life. Not that he'd have known it *was* teak if Sabrina hadn't told him.

They made their way slowly around the yacht, starting with the master stateroom with its understated elegance, on to the second stateroom, just as elegant but not so large. They stopped in the navigation station, with its teak chart table and upholstered cream-colored leather cushions, an impressive mounting of electronic displays and a downright jovial captain.

The kitchen—Sabrina called it a galley, naturally—had everything from walk-in refrigerators to microwaves and even a barbecue: electric, but a barbecue nonetheless. "Sea rails" around the four-burner gas stove were self-explanatory. The supply of hot and cold water wasn't, until Sabrina pointed out the two-foot pumps.

They even invaded Lucretia's office, where she worked at a teak desk amid a full communications setup that included a telex, a fax, copier, computer and printer.

When Charlie had seen it all, Sabrina pressed her arm against his to get his attention, but she kept her gaze out to sea. "You were impressed," she suggested softly.

"Who wouldn't be?" He gave an impatient snort.

"I knew stuff like this existed, but mere mortals don't get much chance to see it up close and personal."

"It's only stuff," she stated reasonably.

"To you. But you were born to the purple, so to speak, and raised with all this."

"Do you hold it against me?"

She sounded so plaintive that he had to laugh. Straightening away from the rail, he turned toward her. "No, but—"

The yacht lurched and somehow he found her in his arms, looking up at him with wide, brown eyes, lips parted softly. Time stood still; they might have gone from choppy seas to a sea as smooth as glass for all the impact their surroundings had on him.

She licked her lips and she was so close that he could see the shine. "I'm glad you don't hold it against me," she murmured. "I really had nothing to do with it. Remind me to tell you someday...."

He knew he should stand her on her feet and turn her loose; he really should. Instead, he sucked in a deep breath, feeling the soft pressure of her breasts against his chest, the stronger thrust of her hips and thighs against his. Damn, she was a sweet armful. If he kissed her—

"Say something, Malcolm," she whispered, sliding one arm up his shoulder and twining her fingers around his neck. She exerted a subtle pressure. "Say something...or do something...."

"I'll do something al—"

"Malcolm! Sabrina! Don't you hear the dinner bell? Where *are* you two?"

They sprang apart, exchanging guilty glances as if they'd been caught at the Hot Bed Motel. Another five seconds and Lucretia might have gotten the shock of her life.

Thank you, Lucy, Malcolm thought fervently. If there was one thing he didn't need, it was to get mixed up with the daughter of the boss from hell—and have her know about it to boot.

THEY ATE DINNER on the deck beneath a rippling canopy, served by a smiling steward. Charley was so knocked out by his surroundings that he was having trouble concentrating on the food, delicious as it was: roast tenderloin of beef with herb pepper crust, red wine sauce and grilled portobello mushrooms with all the go-withs.

Not his favorite go-withs, of course. Coleslaw and beans would definitely be out of place on china plates set off by the snowy linen tablecloth. And instead of beer, the drink-of-the-day around here seemed to be champagne.

Expensive champagne.

Jeez! If the folks at the orphanage could see him now....

"More champagne, sir?"

"Why...not?"

Lucretia looked at him with the eyes of a hawk or some such predator. "Enjoying yourself, Malcolm?"

"What's not to enjoy?" He stared at the golden bubbles rising in the crystal flute, trying to shake the feeling of unreality clouding his vision and muddling his brain. He had to keep reminding himself that none of this counted. He couldn't start liking it.

"How true." She dropped her snowy napkin on the table and rose. "We'll be landing on Addison Island around nine o'clock. I told them to have the lodge ready, but you never know. We may end up having to rough it tonight."

Charley watched her walk away. "Roughing it? Not Lucretia."

Sabrina smiled. "You might be surprised," she said archly.

"Anything's possible," Charley admitted. "Your mother's the first person I've ever known who had a yacht and a private island. And an airplane—can't forget the airplane."

Sabrina sighed. "Things, just things. They mean very little to her."

He lifted his head and looked her in the eye. "What do they mean to you? You've never been without them."

She cocked her head, a slight frown marring the perfect skin between her perfect eyebrows revealed by wispy brown bangs. "That's true. But I'm not shallow enough to value material things above what's really important."

"Such as?" Maybe the champagne was getting to him. This really wasn't a line of questioning he'd be wise to pursue.

"Honesty." She waved the word like a proud banner, as if she'd invented the concept. "Truth."

The woman was a broken record on the subject. Charley finished his champagne and put the flute on the table, determined to change the subject. "Tell me about your mother's island," he suggested. "I thought most of the Channel Islands were pretty barren places."

"Many of them are, but not ours—I mean hers. The

times I've been there it's been green and glorious. It has a little bit of everything, actually—cliffs and coves and sandy beaches...rocks and tidepools.''

Leaning back in his comfortable leather sling chair, Charley listened to her mellow voice describing wonders he'd never expected to see.

''There's also considerable pasture land. Lucretia has a cattle company there, mostly to provide work for the cowboys who came with the island when she inherited it.'' She smiled suddenly and charmingly. ''When I was a little girl, they taught me to ride the horses and let me pretend I was a real cowgirl. Do you ride?''

''No.''

''Want to learn?''

It hung in the air between them, an invitation to become even more intimately involved with this maddening but beautiful—and out-of-bounds—woman. A lot depended upon his answer.

Charley got to his feet. ''I'm here to work, not to have a good time.''

Sabrina laughed. ''Go on, Malcolm. *You* know and *I* know that Lucretia brought you along to keep me from going so crazy with boredom that I'd bail out before the coronation.''

''Yeah, you're right.'' He glowered at her. ''So what do you want from me, Your Highness?''

LUCRETIA'S ''LODGE'' turned out to be a country castle on a bluff overlooking the ocean. Charley had never seen anything like it. It gleamed in the sunlight as if it were made of pearl. The gardens and terraces that surrounded it were equally perfect, so perfect that none of it seemed any more real than the trip over.

This place even put Sabrina's Santa Barbara villa in the shade.

Breakfast was served in his room, although he hadn't requested it. When the maid carried in the tray, he wondered aloud about such service.

"The ladies usually have breakfast in bed while they're here," she explained cheerfully. "Mrs. Hodges, the housekeeper, thought you might prefer that to eating alone in the dining room."

He did. The coffee in the silver server was delicious, the bacon crispy just the way he liked it, the pancakes light and fluffy. He'd just dug into the fresh fruit, when his bedroom door flew open without preamble.

Dressed only in his boxers, he made a dive for his clothes.

"Oh, give it up, Malcolm," Lucretia said. "You haven't got anything I haven't seen before."

"Yeah, but you haven't seen it on me and I'd just as soon keep it that way." He jammed his legs into jeans and stood up, buttoning the fly. "Jeez," he grumbled, "you're my employer, for—"

"All right, all right, don't get your shorts in a knot." She gave him a devilish smile, which quickly slipped into a frown. "Malcolm, I'm appalled," she added.

"By what?" Feeling defensive, he sat back down before his breakfast tray.

She did not look pleased. "You're a...damn, you're a kind of a hunk." She fluttered her fingers toward his bare chest. "I certainly hope Sabrina hasn't seen you like this," she added with disapproval.

He took instant offense. "Like what?"

"Practically naked."

"Naked!" He looked down at his bare chest, then glared at her. "I know this is your house, but is this my room or not?"

"Of course it is, Malcolm. For a while, anyway." Wandering over, she plucked a grape from the bowl on his breakfast tray.

"Then as long as it's my room, I don't want anybody barging in without knocking. You got that?"

"My, my, aren't we getting testy. What do you expect to be doing in here that your mother couldn't see?"

"I don't have a mother. If I did, she wouldn't be you." He tried not to shudder.

If she saw, she didn't let on. "I stand corrected," she said airily. "Now, answer my question. Has Sabrina seen…the real you? The rippling muscles, the bulging pecs? Tell me you haven't inflicted such a sight upon her innocent eyes."

Finally she made him laugh. "Relax, Lucy. Sabrina isn't in the habit of busting into my bedroom without knocking."

"I don't want her in here even if she does knock, you got that? She doesn't have time for a fling with my assistant. When she leaves this island I expect it to be as an engaged woman."

"You don't have to get insulting." He shoved back the tray, appetite gone.

"Insulting?" She rolled her eyes. "That's trivial, compared with what's at stake here. Do we understand each other? I do *not* want my daughter to see you without your clothes on."

"Then I'll try to resist any urges to tear off my clothes when she's around," he muttered.

"Good. Bonus intact." Lucretia turned toward the door. "Feel free to get on with your assignment. I want you to keep Bree from getting too bored while I whip this party into shape."

"'Whip' being the operative word."

She gave him a conspiratorial wink. "I expect you to tell me everything, of course. And I do mean everything."

"I won't spy for you."

"Of course you will. It's your job." With a flutter of fingers, she hastened from the room, leaving one very disgusted individual behind her.

FOR TWO DAYS, Charley let Sabrina drag him all over the island. They looked over the cattle operation, explored the beaches, tromped over the bluffs and valleys while she regaled him with stories of the island's history.

"How'd you learn so much about this place?" he asked on the second day, when they'd paused on craggy cliffs overlooking the pounding surf below. "You're a veritable fount of information."

She grinned, looking adorable in her jeans and mint green T-shirt, silky hair pulled back in a careless ponytail. "You remember meeting José?" she asked.

Charley thought for a moment. "One of the cowboys. The old one, right?"

She nodded. A slight breeze from the water stirred curly tendrils of hair that had escaped the rubber band holding the rest of it back. "José's part Indian and he's spent his entire life here. When I was little, he used to tell me stories, wonderful stories about his people.''

''Tell me,'' he said, just to keep her talking. Watching those full lips form words was turning into a major delight.

''Well, the Chumash Indians have been in these islands for more than six thousand years. When Juan Rodriguez Cabrillo got here in 1542, he was a regular Johnny-come-lately.''

Charley was impressed. ''I never could remember history dates,'' he told her.

She shrugged modestly, as if it were nothing. ''I've never found that a problem. Ask me anything.''

''Uh...'' He pondered about a question. ''When did the Civil War start?''

She laughed. ''Everybody knows that. Think of something harder?''

When did I start falling in love with Sabrina Addison?

That was harder, all right. Charley's stomach flip-flopped in protest.

''What's the matter?'' she asked. ''You look absolutely green, all of a sudden.''

''I'm fine,'' he croaked, not feeling fine at all. ''Think we should head on back?''

''Oh, no. You're not feeling well.'' She scooted off the rock on which she sat, sinking down onto the grassy hill. She patted her lap. ''Here, lie down and rest your head. I'll rub your temples and you'll feel better soon.''

He'd feel better when this cockamamy scheme of Lucretia's was played out. ''No, thanks,'' he said. ''I'm feeling better already.''

"In that case—" she jumped up, brushing off the seat of her jeans and drawing his unwilling attention to a neat little rear end "—we can go on down and see if I can remember how to find that cave. José told me it was used by pirates a long time ago. Who knows, Malcolm? Maybe we'll find something precious down there."

Or maybe we won't, he grumbled as he followed her down the cliff toward the beach. *Maybe all we'll find is trouble.*

MALCOLM WASN'T HAPPY.

He was following her with a scowl, as if he didn't really want to be here at all. If she didn't know better, that could have hurt her feelings. But she did know better. Malcolm was attracted to her, whether he wanted to admit it or not.

She led the way along the beach, narrow here and rocky. Foamy waves lapped at her sneakers, but the sun was warm overhead and she didn't care if her feet got wet. To her left, rocky cliffs towered over all, making her feel small if not insignificant.

She stopped suddenly and he ran into her with a soft exclamation of surprise. His arms went around her quite naturally, and instead of stepping away, she leaned back against him, surprised by the hardness of his body against hers. She'd never thought Malcolm was a particularly buff individual. Cute, yes, but not a hunk.

He released her and jumped back somewhat belatedly. "What is it?" he wanted to know, his voice under pressure.

Heaven knows it wasn't *her* fault. She pointed. "I think that's it." Grabbing his hand, she started toward the sea cave, formed by the incessant wind-driven sand on this section of the island.

For a moment he held back, but then he was running lightly beside her, splashing through the low surf to reach the entrance to the cave. His eyes, as blue as the ocean, sparkled with an interest he couldn't hide from her.

His grin revealed those perfect white teeth. "Pirates, you say?"

"Pirates, José said."

He glanced around. "I can see them crossing swords on the beach there, under the popular theory that dead men tell no tales."

She stepped up close to him. "I have a few theories of my own."

He took a step back, a look almost of panic crossing his face. "Such as?"

She reached out to toy with the top button of his chambray shirt. Gosh, it was nice the way it strained to cover his chest when he sucked in a big, anxious-sounding breath.

"For one thing, I believe we should act on what we're feeling."

"Ohhhh, boy. Not a good idea."

His top button popped open and at almost the same moment he covered her hand with his and swung it wide.

So she used her other hand to open his second button, thrusting out her lower lip in calculated concentration. "I also believe we should be honest about our feelings," she murmured.

He covered her second hand with his second hand and swung that arm wide, too, until they stood there facing each other, touching where their hands met. "You're bigger on honesty than anyone I've ever met," he conceded. "Okay, Sabrina, try this bit of honesty on for size. If your mother thought I was messing with you, she'd not only fire me, she'd cut off a few of my most interesting parts and mount them on her trophy wall."

Sabrina laughed incredulously, then stepped forward adroitly to press her pliant body against his rigid one, shoulder to knee. "You expect me to believe you're afraid of my mother?" she purred. "Not a big, strong man like you...Malcolm. Be honest...be honest with me...."

Now he's going to give in, she thought smugly. He was going to take her in his arms and kiss her silly and then...and then...who knows what?

She was wrong. He jerked away from her as if he'd been jabbed by a cattle prod, then faced her with blue eyes blazing.

"You want honest?" he snarled.

She blinked in bewilderment. "Of course. My goodness, Malcolm, what's got you so upset?"

"I'm not Malcolm!"

She laughed. "Then who are you, his evil twin?"

"No!" He flung himself around, bracing one hand against the stony entrance to the cave. "My name is Charley Lawrence."

"But— I thought you were joking before! Lucretia's assistants have always been named..." Understanding dawned. "Of course! That's what she calls them. I'm an idiot!" She struck herself a glancing blow on the side of the head. "Not even Lucretia could find five guys in a row named Malcolm to work for her.''

"Damn straight." He turned back to face her cautiously. His shirt, unfastened two buttons down, gaped just enough for her to get a glance at the firm golden flesh teasingly revealed. "I'm a real person—surprise! I'm not made of steel—surprise! I actually have feelings—surprise!''

"Of course you do.'' Indignant for what her mother had put him through, Sabrina laid a comforting hand on his forearm.

He yanked away. "You think I'm just your mother's yes-man,'' he accused.

"The thought crossed my mind, but that was before I got to know you,'' she said earnestly, crowding him back toward the beach deliberately. "Now I think of you as my friend, Mal—Charley.''

"You do?''

"Of course I do.''

He seemed to pull himself together with an effort. "Don't. Don't think of me as your friend or anything else. There's no future in it, Sabrina. I've got my life and you've got yours and never the twain shall meet.''

"I'm not so sure you're right about that,'' she purred, holding his gaze with hers. She slid both hands up his arms until they rested on his shoulders. He felt as tight as a drum, explosive almost. Very satisfying, actually. "Charley—''

"Don't, Sabrina.'' His voice was thick, heavy. "Don't go on. You'll regret it if you do.''

"I hardly ever regret anything,'' she said truthfully. "In fact, the only things I remember with regret are the things I *didn't* do...." She licked her lips, slowly, deliberately provocative. *What did she have to do, draw him a picture?*

"Okay, then," he said self-righteously. "Don't say I didn't warn you."

And he gave her a caveman yank into his arms and kissed her.

Finally.

SHE KISSED HIM back. Damn! If she'd slapped his face, everything would have been all right. But did she have the decency to do that? Hell, no!

Everything could have been all right at any point along the way to this moment if she'd just remembered her place. But, no, she had to get all democratic about it, calling him "Charley" and licking those luscious lips with her little red tongue, all but asking for his forgiveness.

Now here they were, hip to hip and breast to chest. She didn't wait for him to part her lips with his tongue, didn't wait for him to enter that sweet cavern. The woman had no restraint whatsoever. With lips sweet and ripe as some exotic fruit, she met him more than halfway.

As one, they dropped to their knees on the beach, never breaking the contact of their mouths. As one, they sank onto their sides in the sand, still wrapped in each other's arms and lost in a kiss that threatened to go on and on forever.

With one hand he touched her face, feeling the smooth skin like an aphrodisiac beneath his fingers. With the other hand he stroked her breast, tugged at her shirt—

And nearly choked her with his grip when a surge of water washed over them on its way to the shore— cold, frigid water that stole breath and restored reason. With a yelp of disbelief, Charley sprang to his feet, hauling her up with him.

Her ponytail dripped seawater. Her cotton knit shirt clung to her breasts, outlining nipples taut with cold or Charley's touch. He hoped like hell it was the latter. She stared at him and he was too ensnared in his emotions to read hers.

But whatever came next, he wasn't going to like it. She might do anything: slap his face or laugh in it, cry, run screaming to her mother. He'd totally overstepped himself this time. Bye-bye, Kansas City.

She pushed escaping tendrils of hair away from her face and smiled. "Gee, Charley," she said in a low, sexy voice. "I've wanted to try that ever since I saw *From Here to Eternity* on the late late show. It was...nice."

"Nice? Nice!" Charley thrust his hands through his hair, shoving the wet locks out of his eyes and trying to think straight. "Deborah Kerr and Burt Lancaster must have frozen their patooties off making that scene. It *wasn't* nice. It was...it was—"

When he couldn't come up with a word, she offered helpfully, "Wonderful? Fabulous? Sensational?"

"Insane!"

"Really, you exaggerate." Catching his hand in hers, she lifted it to her cheek. "Why don't we find some less...exposed location and give it another try?"

"Are you crazy?" He yanked his hand away and backed up a few steps.

"Crazy?" She frowned. "Why would you say that?"

"I've got to spell it out for you?" He sucked in a deep breath meant to steady him. "This is an absolute dead end for me, Sabrina."

She dimpled. "Not necessarily."

He groaned. "You know what I mean. You must. You're a pretty princess with a mother from hell, remember? That mother is also my boss and has my future by the balls."

Her laughter was explosive. "You have quite a manner of speaking, Charley."

"But you know what I mean. This—" he indicated the two of them "—is *not* a good idea."

"I think it's a swell idea." She glided toward him. "If she fires you, I'll hire you."

"Out of the frying pan," he said darkly. "It's not that simple and you know it."

"It should be." He retreated; she stopped, a frown creating cute little creases between her eyebrows. "Will you stop running away from me? I know you don't find me…repulsive…."

He groaned long and loud.

She bestowed an angelic smile upon him. "And I don't find you repulsive, either. I'm not saying this will go anywhere, but it seems to me that the least we can do is find out."

He shook his head stubbornly. "I've got too much to lose."

"What, besides your job?"

He was desperate; if she laid one more hand on

him he was going to be on her like perfume on a rose. "My dream, Sabrina. I've got my dream to lose."

That rocked her. He supposed it wasn't politically correct to trash a person's dream for the sake of a quick tumble, and she was nothing if not PC.

She looked at him with a face filled with sympathy and understanding. "Then you must tell me all about it," she said. "Gosh, Mal—Charley, I feel as if we're really getting to know each other now."

Which was the last thing in the world he wanted— make that next to the last. The *last* thing was for Lucretia to find out about this. Ah, hell, who was he kidding? The last, the very last, thing he wanted was to betray or disappoint this shining, wonderful creature who looked at him as if his dream must be as epic as her imagination.

"A BARBECUE RESTAURANT? You want to go back to Kansas City and open a *barbecue* restaurant?" She could hardly believe her ears. He was passing up the possibility of...*really* getting to know her for a slab of ribs and a dollop of sticky red sauce? She'd never been so insulted in her life!

But then she looked past her pique and into his blue, blue eyes and saw that this was of supreme importance to him. She had no idea why, but it was.

He nodded miserably. "I know it must be hard for you to understand. You've had so much, I don't suppose this makes any sense. But it's what I'm good at, Bree. It's what I've wanted since I was just a kid." He held a flat hand a few feet off the ground to illustrate.

"But, Charley," she objected softly, "why is it

mutually exclusive? Can't you let nature take its course and still have your barbecue restaurant?''

"What would be the point?" He looked really vulnerable when he said it. "We couldn't possibly mean anything *important* to each other. If there was a chance of that…well, then everything would be different. But you're a poor little rich girl and I'm a poor little poor boy and it's best we keep our distance from here on out."

She laughed incredulously. "You're kidding."

"The hell I am!" He looked outraged that she'd suggest it.

"In that case…" Slowly she rose from her seat on a rock at the edge of the beach and brushed sand from her jeans. "I've got to think about this, Charley."

"There's nothing to think about, Sabrina."

"Oh, I don't know." She gave him an oblique glance. "That kiss was pretty powerful."

He groaned. "It should never have happened and never will again. I apologize. Forget all about it."

"I don't believe I ever got an apology for a kiss before," she said. "I'm not sure I like it."

"That's the spirit. Get mad. I deserve it." He looked relieved. Turning, he started back up the beach. "It's getting late," he said without looking back at her. "We'd better head back to the house before Lucy sends out the dogs."

She watched him walk away, measuring his tall figure while thinking thoughts at once scornful and strangely tender. His name was Charley. She shivered, suddenly struck by the intimacy of it all. He wasn't Malcolm at all. He was a totally different person from the one she'd thought he was.

How horrible she'd been! What had he accused her of, treating those around her like minions? She'd thought the charge insane, but now she saw he'd been telling the truth. She'd certainly treated *him* like a minion, a minion named Malcolm. But underneath that quiet exterior lurked a hunk named Charley.

He'd been right and she'd been wrong, but Sabrina Addison was nothing if not willing to face up to her inadequacies, no matter how few. She'd make it up to him, whether he liked it or not—but of course he would.

Grinning, Sabrina followed him to the path up the cliffs. This wasn't over, not by a long shot. But she had no problem with letting him lull himself into a false sense of security.

When the time was right…

LUCRETIA PACED back and forth on the veranda, obviously waiting for them. "Oh, bother!" Sabrina said, sounding cranky. "I'm in no mood for another go-around with *her!*"

Charley wasn't, either. He glanced down at his crumpled clothing, dry now, but stiff with salt and smelly with ocean water. His skin felt crusty and tight and his hair was probably standing on end.

If it wasn't it should be, after that harrowing escape. He stole a glance at Sabrina and found her just as gorgeous as ever, her skin apparently impervious to the elements and her crumpled clothing an almost delightful contrast to the fine frame it concealed. Little tendrils from her ponytail curled around her face, lending an air of vulnerability to her beauty.

He wanted to groan his frustration, but gritted his

teeth against it. He'd said his say and that was that. For one wild, brief moment she'd been his for the asking, but that memory would now fade to an unattainable dream.

He devoutly hoped.

Lucretia met them at the steps, looking crisp and elegant in slacks and a royal-blue silk shirt. Her perfectly cool chic made him feel even grubbier, if that was possible.

"Good Lord, what happened to you two?" she demanded. "You look like you've been sleeping in those clothes—or worse."

Sabrina glared at her mother. "I don't think that's any of your—"

"We got caught in the surf," Charley butted in, not up for another mother-daughter cat fight. "If you don't mind, I'll go on up and change before dinner."

"I do mind," Lucretia said bluntly. She didn't look as if she found particular credence in his explanation. She licked her lips, revealing an unexpected anxiety. "There's something I need to tell my daughter," she said with a reluctance that was palpable.

Charley felt relief. "In that case, why don't I—"

Sabrina grabbed his arm, cutting off his reasoned request for dismissal, touching him as if she owned him. All he needed was for Lucretia to get suspicious and it was goodbye Kansas City barbecue!

His fears, however, did not transmit themselves magically to the woman clinging to his arm. "I want you here," Sabrina said, glaring at her mother. "Whatever you have to say, Lucretia, *he* can hear, too."

"That's what I had in mind," Lucretia said dryly. "We may need a referee after I...confess all."

"What have you done?"

Lucretia sucked in a deep breath. "There's not going to be a gigantic birthday party, Sabrina. I'm sorry, dear. That was a hoax."

Charley felt icy fear claw its way up his backbone. What in the hell was the woman up to? With his gaze on Sabrina, he saw her flinch and those remarkable brown eyes open wider.

"Then what is this all about?" she asked. "Why did you move heaven and earth to get me here?"

"Because there *will* be a party, a small and intimate gathering with only three guests. All are suitors for your hand, if you'll forgive an antiquated turn of phrase."

"I don't believe this!" Sabrina shook her head. "It's too bizarre."

"Not at all, dear." Lucretia cast a frazzled glance at Charley as if seeking his support—or at least, his understanding. "All three are already in love with you, but you've locked yourself away like a princess in a tower at El Dorado. I thought...well," she argued, "I thought they deserved their chance. You're not getting any younger, you know."

"Who have you involved in your machinations?" Sabrina clenched her hands at her sides and glared at her mother.

"Don't be angry, sweetheart. I've invited Brigg Newton—"

"Jeez," Charley muttered, "you've invited a cookie?"

Lucretia sent him a swift, scorching glance of rebuttal. "That's *Brigg,* not *fig.*"

Sabrina hugged his arm tighter, one firm breast crushed against him and more or less wiping out his global awareness.

"How dare you speak to him that way?" she cried.

Lucretia rolled her eyes. "Malcolm doesn't mind. We understand each other, which is more than I can say for— Never mind. To continue, the other two are Jordan Longmont and Teddy Thorpe."

Sabrina clenched her teeth. "I hope they won't be disappointed when I'm not here."

Lucretia looked almost regretful. "But you will be, darling, because I'm not letting you off this island until you give them a chance to woo you and win you."

"You can't keep me here against my will!" Sabrina cried. "That's—that's kidnapping!" She appealed to Charley. "Can she?"

"Hell, I don't know," he admitted. "Probably." Knowing Lucretia, he was sure of it.

Lucretia tried to soothe her distraught daughter. "It's only for a week," she said. "All you have to do is give them a chance. They're fine young men, Bree, all three of them—perfect gentlemen of your own...forgive me, but of your own class. All you have to do is relax, have fun, see if anything... develops. If at the end of the week your answer is still no, I swear I'll accept it." She held up her hands in a gesture of mock surrender.

Not even Charley believed her.

"Will you put that in writing?" Sabrina asked through gritted teeth.

"Absolutely."

"I don't suppose when you say 'give them a chance' that means I've got to sleep with them?"

"Sabrina!" Lucretia clutched at her throat as if she'd been struck a mortal blow. "How can you talk that way to your mother?" She spared a glance at Charley. "And in front of *him!*"

Sabrina's laughter sounded brittle, defeated. "Little do you know, Lucretia. Little do you know...."

7

CHARLEY FOUND dinner a depressing affair. At its conclusion, he was glad to escape to his room and a good book selected from the library. Unfortunately, he was unable to concentrate, and after reading the first page three or four times, he gave up and wandered out onto the balcony overlooking the ocean.

How did people live like this and still remember their basic humanity? He'd heard it said that "power corrupts and absolute power corrupts absolutely." Maybe it was also true that "luxury corrupts and absolute luxury corrupts absolutely." If so, who was he—a poor boy *not* from the wrong side of the tracks but from a place that didn't even *have* tracks—to condemn?

What was Lucretia trying to do, sell her daughter to the highest bidder? A protective wave of indignation swept over him and he fought it down. Sabrina was no helpless hothouse flower, no matter what she or her mother thought. Sabrina could take care of herself. Sabrina...

He took off his clothes and climbed into bed, thinking of Sabrina...and what had happened between them on the beach...and what *might* have happened without that cold dose of saltwater reality.

WHEN HE WOKE UP who knows how much later, she was in the bed beside him whispering urgently in his ear.

"Charley, Charley, are you awake?"

The voice registered faintly, overwhelmed by a multitude of stronger sensations....

A bedroom brilliantly illuminated by a crystal spill of moonlight through open French doors...a whiff of roses, heady and erotic in its intensity...a feather-light touch on his shoulders...

A faint stirring of warm breath against his ear and words at once soothing and urgent: "Please, Charley, it's me, Sabrina. I've got to talk to you."

With a languorous sigh, Charley turned his head to look at her. She lay beside him on his bed, he beneath the sheet and she on top of it. She wore something short and pale, her nipples dark beneath the sheer fabric. He swallowed hard, rattled by the unexpectedness of it all, the unreality.

Maybe it *was* unreal. Maybe he was still dreaming. He tested his voice with a single croaking word: "Sabrina?"

Her soft laughter jangled through him. "Of course. Who else could it be?" Leaning close, she planted a quick kiss on his cheek. "Charley, you've got to save me!"

"Save—" He swallowed hard. He felt paralyzed with unreality. "Save you from what?"

"From Lucretia and her crazy schemes." She snuggled against his arm, curving her cheek to his bare shoulder. She slid one arm across his chest right at the line of demarcation provided by the sheet. "You've got to help me get away from here."

He tried to think about what she was saying, but the light scraping of her nails across his chest, just above the sheet, distracted him. "Uhh..." he said with considerable effort, "if you're thinking of swimming out you'd better think again."

She laughed and pressed her mouth just below his collarbone as if to stifle the sound. "You're funny."

His skin burned where she'd touched it. "Believe me, that wasn't my intent."

She sighed rapturously. "Thank God I have you to turn to, Charley. It's all that's keeping me sane."

"Come on, Sabrina." He felt sweat breaking out on his forehead. She was really putting the screws to him here, inadvertently or not. "She's worried about you. She promised if you'd do this for her, she'd leave you alone."

"You can't believe her."

She sounded so mournful that he felt obliged to drag his arm from beneath her and slip it around her waist, just as a point of comfort. "She said she'd put it in writing."

She rubbed her cheek back and forth over his shoulder, somehow managing to slip down to his chest. She dropped a quick kiss just south of his nipple. "She's still playing games with my head. She's always lied to me, my entire life." She slipped her left hand down over his taut belly, on top of the sheet. "I can't believe anything she says. She's trying to control me and she'll cheat and finagle to get her way. She—"

"Stop it!" He wasn't sure if he meant stop talking or stop groping. He grabbed the wrist of the errant hand and lifted it from his body.

She blinked up at him, her expression vulnerable. "Charley! I thought I could count on you." That delicious lower lip trembled slightly.

So clenched up he could hardly breathe, Charley struggled to bring his mind to bear on the problem at hand, which should be the relationship between this mother and daughter, but wasn't.

"You can count on me," he grated, "but not to tell you you're right when you're not."

"I don't understand," she murmured plaintively, managing to slide her wrist from his grasp. "I thought we were friends."

"We are friends, Sabrina, or as close to friends as is possible under the circumstances." Sweating bullets, he stared at the pattern of moonlight on the wall behind her, lacy and mysterious, determined not to look at the body shimmering beneath a nightgown as sheer as the moonlight.

"What circumstances?"

She slid her knee over his thigh and hooked her heel beneath his calf, wiggling closer. She was like a little girl seeking comfort, or like a big girl seeking...something else.

He cleared his throat, willing himself to rise above the pressure of her knee in a most sensitive area of his anatomy. "This is between you and your mother," he stated. "You're going to have to work it out between you."

"Can't be done. I'll never believe—"

"Damn it, Sabrina!" Something in him snapped, but he wasn't sure if it was caused by the mental or physical anguish she was unknowingly inflicting upon his unprepared self. "So what? Life isn't perfect. At least your mother loves you, which is a lot more than some people get."

"Charley! You yelled at me."

"I'm sorry, but you're driving me crazy." In every imaginable way.

"I can't let you go on thinking that I'm nothing but a spoiled rich girl." She rolled over him, hiking herself up on her arms, half on him and half on the bed. She looked into his eyes, hers appealing. The ends of her unbound hair tickled his chest.

He tried to look away, but unfortunately his fugitive gaze went down instead of up. The filmy gown gaped, fully exposing perfect breasts already peaking. His mouth went dry.

"Sabrina…" It was a pitiful groan.

She remained undeterred. "Because I value your opinion so much, Charley, I'm going to tell you my deepest, darkest secret."

"I don't think I want to know."

"You told me your dream, so I can trust you with my secret."

"That could…be a mistake. I wouldn't trust me if I were you."

She forged ahead. "I only found this out a year ago." Her voice sounded choked, almost edged with tears. "It ruined my last birthday party."

She settled down until she straddled his thigh. It was all he could do to lie still. "I…heard something about that," he admitted. "But no one seemed to know what had happened."

"Charley, I'm adopted!" It was a cry of anguish.

For a moment he just lay there, trying to take it all

in. "You mean, you only found this out a year ago? Lucretia isn't your real mother?"

"Yes! Did you ever hear anything so horrible? She lied to me! My entire life, she lied to me. She made me think she was someone she wasn't! It's too awful." Dropping onto his chest, she trembled with reaction to this terrible tale of betrayal.

If she expected sympathy from Charley Lawrence—and she obviously did—he was going to have to disillusion her in a hurry. He slid his hands to her shoulders, fought off the desire to gather her even closer and instead gave her a little shake. "Get a grip, Sabrina!"

"Do what?" She twisted her head around so she could see his face, her own expression and tone disbelieving. "I'm adopted, Charley, and the truth was kept from me by that woman. What do you *mean*, get a grip?"

"I mean it's not the end of the world. It's not even a hanging offense."

"Well, maybe it should be!"

She tried to struggle upright, but he wouldn't let her go, which meant all her wiggles and gyrations brought him new agonies. "Hold still," he gasped. "I can't talk when you're...doing that."

"I don't want you to talk!" She struggled harder. "Not anymore. You've betrayed me, Charley. Is there no one I can trust?"

At his wit's end and bereft of options, he flipped her over onto her back and held her there with his aching body. Her face in the moonlight revealed shock and then she caught her breath and turned her head away. For the first time he realized that one of her hands was fisted, as if she were hiding something. Well, let her. Let her keep her secrets. *He* sure as hell didn't want to know anymore.

"Sabrina," he said, "I was an orphan myself, so don't try to tell me that being adopted by one of the richest women on God's green earth is some terrible hardship. It's not."

She gasped and jerked her head around so she could look at him again. "You were? Oh, Charley! Were you adopted by a nice family?"

"I wasn't adopted at all," he said grimly. "I got bounced around to foster homes and even spent some time in an institution, which is what they call orphanages now."

"Then you know how I feel," she whispered. "Why, we have something in common after all!"

"Are you nuts? You grew up in the lap of luxury with a mother who dotes on you and I grew up with strangers. You call that something in common?"

"But—"

"But me no buts, Sabrina. You're nuts to look good fortune in the mouth."

"What good fortune?"

"Lucretia's love and money and generosity, that's what good fortune. Sheesh!" He released her and sat up, only belatedly realizing the sheet had come unfurled in the proceedings. Hastily he yanked it over his lap.

"But—"

"Lucretia may show her love in inappropriate ways," he pressed on, "but so what? That's part of her charm, when you come to think about it."

"You think she's got charm?" Sabrina followed

him, on her elbows. Almost casually she slid one hand beneath the sheet draped over his lap.

Her hand touched his bare thigh and he flinched, "Yes!" bursting from his lips. He added hastily, "I mean yes, she's got a certain *charm!*" He blurted out the last word when her wandering hand found what she apparently sought and settled in to work magic.

"So you're telling me...?" Her voice was a purr of satisfaction.

"To...take your mother at face value and stop... sniveling,"

"No one ever talked to me that way except you, Charley Lawrence." She sighed. "That's a brilliant analysis."

Charley licked his lips and tried to think of honor, duty and Kansas City. She just kept doing what she was doing as if waiting for him to notice. Notice? She was killing him! "I...wouldn't exactly call it... brilliant."

"I would." Without releasing her hold on him, she scooted up beside him. "I believe I'll take your advice. I'm going to stop sniveling and...seduce you, Charley Lawrence."

He closed his eyes and prayed for strength. "I'm not prepared. We can't because I can't...I don't have...anything and I'd never... Sabrina, stop that! I'd never...if I could help it—"

"Dear, dear Charley. Open your eyes."

"What?"

"I said, look at what I just happen to have."

He did, but it took considerable effort. With a flourish, she spread the fingers of her closed fist and there, nestled on that soft little palm, was the answer to a desperate man's prayer. Make that a desperate, *shocked* man's prayer. She seemed so innocent that premeditation hadn't even occurred to him. Now that it had—

He shoved his hands into the satin softness of her hair as he'd so often longed to do and brought her face close to his. "Sabrina, you're out of your mind in more ways than one," he said. "But what the hell? I'm a touch crazed at the moment myself."

"Charley, you talk too much," she said, and lifted her lips to his.

SABRINA, who'd known exactly what she wanted when she slipped into his bed wearing little more than a smile and her favorite perfume, was more than happy to let him take the initiative.

My goodness, she thought hazily, arching, stretching like a cat; Charley is *powerful!* Who'd ever have thought that beneath his calm demeanor, behind those deceitful glasses, lurked a tiger?

"Sabrina...?"

She heard the strangled note in the way he said her name, as if he could barely force it out. She smiled. "Yes, Charley?" She slid her fingers through his tousled hair and hung on.

"This..." He was struggling. "Doesn't change anything. It...can't."

"Charley, dear—" She shifted, lifted, found. "It changes...everything."

"Sabrina—"

And then he must have discovered that what she said was true, for he stopped talking and became the man of action she'd known instinctively he would be.

SHE LAY EXHAUSTED in his bed, breathing hard and staring up at the ceiling with its slowly rotating fan. Sheer curtains over the French doors stirred and billowed into the room, fragile in their beauty.

Sabrina knew how they felt. She, too, felt fragile, not so much physically as emotionally. She had given Charley everything, and to her surprise, he had given everything back and then some.

Turning her head, she looked at him beside her on the silky smooth cotton sheets. He lay with a forearm over his eyes, as if he couldn't bear to relinquish the magic.

She smiled. Of course, there was always the chance he might be reluctant to face what had just happened, but she doubted that. Oh, yes, she doubted it!

She kissed his shoulder and he started as if she'd bitten him. "Charley," she whispered, wanting to give him something for what he'd given her, "I'll try to follow your advice."

"What advice?"

"You know, about Lucretia."

"Oh, that." He said it as if he'd been thinking about something completely different.

"I'll try to be more tolerant," she promised. "Maybe you're right. Maybe I should be grateful instead of resentful. I'll take a crack at it and see where it goes."

Rolling over, she sat up on the side of the bed. As much as she longed to remain beside him, she knew she was courting disaster. If Lucretia found them together—she shuddered. Lucretia wouldn't do anything to *her* but Charley would be in imminent danger of death or dismemberment.

"I've got to go," she said, hoping he'd object.

He turned sharply toward her, rolling over and reaching out to curve one hand around her bare hip. "Don't—" His grip tightened possessively, then relaxed, drew away. "Don't let me keep you. Damnation!" He slid his hand around her waist and slipped it between her thighs. "We can't let this happen again, Sabrina."

Now she was the one having trouble talking. "Let what happen?"

He worked his way deeper, found what he sought. "This. We're flirting with disaster. You know that, don't you? We've got to be strong. We can't let it happen again."

"Well..." With a sigh, she leaned back against him on the bed. "Maybe just this once more...."

When she crept out of his room an hour later, she thought she heard him murmuring over and over in the dark, "Kansas City, Kansas City, Kansas City...."

SABRINA'S SUITORS arrived by yacht the following day. When they returned to the house with mother and daughter, Charley was summoned to meet them. He supposed that was Sabrina's idea; Lucretia certainly looked annoyed by the whole thing.

Sabrina smiled and walked on through the room and out the opposite door, headed who knows where. Lucretia did the honors.

The tall, thin, blond guy with the narrow face and worldly expression was Jordan Longmont of Monterey. His handshake was limp, as was his "Pleased to meet you."

The tanned golden boy with the sun-streaked hair and bouncy stride was Teddy Thorpe. His handshake nearly rattled Charley's teeth. "How ya doin', man?" he inquired with a puppy dog's enthusiasm

The third guy brought a frown to Charley's face. Brigg Newton, despite his flaky name, looked almost normal, with the possible exception of all those muscles. On the face of it, he was what women of Charley's acquaintance tended to call tall, dark and handsome. His handshake was firm but not overpowering, his smile apparently genuine.

"Malcolm," he said, white teeth flashing. "So you work with our Lucy. You must be a saint."

"Actually, the name's—"

Lucretia harrumphed. "Don't be impertinent, Brigg. Malcolm is a dedicated young man who is excellent at his job. If there's anything you need and I'm not around, ask him."

Brigg's brows rose. "Instead of Sabrina? She's the reason we're here, right?"

The other two men looked noncommittal; Charley tried not to let his disapproval show. What the hell were they planning to do, hold a lottery with Sabrina as the prize?

Sabrina. Damn, he'd tried every way in the world not to think about her and he hadn't been able to think of anything else. She was under his skin, in his blood. All he could think about was—

"Malcolm!" Lucretia finally got his attention. "I *said,* maybe you and I can get a little work done while our guests settle in."

Sure, why not? Maybe going a couple of rounds with Countess Dracula was just what he needed.

LUCRETIA BROUGHT UP the subject on Charley's mind, sparing him the necessity of casting about for a graceful opening. "So what do you think of Sabrina's three suitors?" she inquired.

Charley worded his reply carefully. "Well...two out of three are nerds."

"Malcolm!" She looked personally affronted.

"Sorry. You asked. Where'd you dig them up, anyway?"

Her sense of humor overrode her indignation. "Here and there. Brigg was our next-door neighbor while Sabrina was growing up in Beverly Hills, if you can call five-acre estates 'next door.'"

"He knows her pretty well, then." Not good. Not good at all.

"Better than anyone," Lucretia said, oblivious to undercurrents in the room. "They've known each other forever. His family adores her."

"Naturally. What about the anyone-for-tennis type?"

She thought for a moment, then said, "Oh, you mean Teddy? He comes from very old money and lots of it. Mostly he spends his time skiing or surfing, depending on the season." She frowned at Charley. "Now, don't look so superior. He can afford it, so why not?"

Charley didn't give a hoot in hell what Teddy did with his bucks, so long as he didn't try to drag Sabrina down to his level. "And the other guy...?"

"Jordan Longmont. His family is in diamonds. Very sophisticated, knows all about wines and horses. He met Sabrina a couple of years ago in Cannes."

Cannes. Just as if that were as natural as, say, Disneyland or the corner grocery store. Sabrina wasn't going to fall for that.

But looking at Sabrina's mother, Charley realized someone else had already fallen for it. Lucretia's eyes glowed with enthusiasm. Still, he heard himself saying a bit defensively, "You don't really think Sabrina's going to pick one of these three, do you?"

"Why wouldn't she?" Lucretia looked astonished he'd even ask. "I want nothing but the best for my little girl, Malcolm." She spoke with utter conviction that couldn't be doubted. "These boys are that—of good family, wealthy and devoted to my daughter. They'll spend their lives trying to make her happy. That's all I ask of a son-in-law—that and grandchildren."

He shook his head slowly. "I don't get it. Where does love enter into all this?"

Lucretia's laughter was like a low, sarcastic comment. "You can't live on love, Malcolm. I know. I tried. That's not good enough for Sabrina." She lifted her chin—actually, thrust it out as if prepared to take a punch. "I came from...crap, Malcolm—let's be honest here. I knew a boy like these three once, the most wonderful boy in the world. Unfortunately—"

She bit her lip and looked away for a moment, finally continuing in a less emotional tone. "Boys like that thought they were too good for me, but now they flock after my daughter," she said proudly. "They'd jump through hoops to win her. When I see them competing for her favor, I remember that boy who broke my heart a lifetime ago and I wish he could see—"

She stopped suddenly, as if she'd just realized how

much she was revealing. She laughed uneasily. "Don't pay any attention to me. I just want to see my child married and settled down with someone to take care of her, since she won't let her mother do it."

"Lucy, she told me what happened."

Her blue eyes widened. "She... told you what?"

"That she's adopted."

"She told you that?" It was an anguished cry. "She's never told anyone. Why would she—"

"I guess she told me because I kept bugging her to give you a break." He wasn't going to mention how intimate conversation...and other things...could get in bed. Meeting her gaze, he saw the vulnerability behind the defiant expression. He went on more gently. "Now I'm trying to get you to give *her* a break. It's obvious you're trying to force-feed Sabrina what you wanted yourself."

"Not at all." She'd recovered from the initial shock but was still shaky. "I'll thank you not to get involved in this, Malcolm. Let's get back to work. Now, as I told you, the London operation is finally in the black—"

Charley tried to concentrate, but all he could think about was Sabrina: where she was, what she was doing and most of all...with whom she was doing it.

8

TEDDY THORPE TOOK Sabrina for a stroll around the gardens following dinner. Eager to get this whole thing over with, she was pleased with the invitation. A glance at Charley revealed nothing; if he was jealous it sure didn't show. Disappointed at his lack of interest, she followed Teddy outside onto the veranda.

They strolled down garden paths, Sabrina playing tour guide. He was, she noticed, quite interested in the time; he checked his Rolex every few minutes. At the twenty-minute mark, he turned suddenly and caught her hands in his.

"Well, enough small talk," he said cheerfully. "Will you marry me, Sabrina? We can travel the world together seeking adventure and thrills. You're the only woman I know who can even come close to keeping up with me." He gave her a broad wink. "Say you will and we'll go break the happy news to your mother."

"Twenty minutes of chitchat and you expect me to fall into your arms? Wham—bam—thank you, ma'am!" She almost felt insulted.

He looked taken aback. "It's not as if we don't already know each other."

"That's true."

"And it's not as if your mother hasn't given me the stamp of approval."

"Don't let it go to your head, Ted. She's given three stamps of approval, actually."

"Oh, them." He shrugged and grinned. "Don't play coy. You know you're nuts about me."

"Bridle your modesty." She put her hands on his shoulders and gazed into his eyes. "Don't you get a sense of déjà vu, here?"

"Should I?"

"Teddy, you proposed to me twice last year, including the last time we met. What makes you think I'd change my mind?"

He frowned. "You mean you haven't?"

"No!" Surprised by her own vehemence, she added, "I adore you, honestly, but I'd make you a terrible wife."

"You wouldn't!"

"I'd certainly try."

He looked confused. "Gosh, Sabrina, when your mother called I thought...and then she said...and when we got here—what the hell, let's go back in and see if we've missed dessert."

Teddy, she mused, was not terribly broken up by her refusal to make his life a living hell.

JORDAN LONGMONT waited a couple of days before making his pitch. In a bad mood because Charley had been avoiding her, Sabrina was less than enthusiastic about agreeing to show Jordan the island. Unfortunately, Lucretia heard his suggestion and barged in, ordering that horses be saddled and a picnic lunch prepared, as well.

They ended up on the cliff overlooking the cave and beach where Charley had first kissed Sabrina— or vice versa; at this point she wasn't sure who'd made the first move. Memories made it hard for her to concentrate, but she tried. When Jordan said her name, she twisted in the saddle, pasting a bright smile on her face.

Reaching into the pocket of his jodhpurs, he withdrew a small jeweler's box, opened it with a flourish and presented it to her. She took it and looked inside.

She'd never seen such an enormous diamond in her life. It was so big and so bright that only belatedly did she realize it was attached to a ring.

"Thanks but no, thanks," she said. Closing the box, she gave it back to him along with a smile.

He looked astonished. "You're not even tempted?"

"By the ring? Hardly." She reached across the space between their horses and patted his cheek. "By you? Unbearably!"

He shrugged, then thrust the box back into his pocket. He looked neither disappointed nor pleased. "It's the Cookie Man, then," he predicted, using Brigg's nickname from his days of athletic glory.

"Why would you say that?" Lifting the reins from her horse's neck, she turned him away from the beach and the memories.

"He's the only one left," Jordan reasoned.

"Oh, no, he's not," Sabrina said before she could stop herself. She added more lightly, "There's plenty of fish in the sea, Jordan."

He gave her an ironic smile. "Not carrying $100,000 diamond rings in their pockets. Ah, well,

Sabrina, I tried. If you change your mind, let me know."

In his dreams.

BRIGG DIDN'T GET around to making his pitch until the fifth day. Naturally, he did it in the swimming pool, where he was practically a fish. Everyone had been swimming earlier—everyone except Charley, of course. With Brigg, a former collegiate diver, showing off, Jordan and Teddy soon found excuses to slink from the field, leaving Sabrina alone with her old friend.

He swam across the pool to where she sat on the edge swinging her legs in the water. His strokes were as powerful and beautiful as his diving, his body more powerful and beautiful than either. Hoisting himself up beside her, he gave her a broad grin, which she returned.

"So," he said cheerfully, "what made your mother think I wanted to marry you?"

She sighed. "Darned if I know, Brigg. She seems to think that every man who ever gazed upon me is smitten." She made a face.

"She's not too far off the mark about that," he said with a chuckle. "But me—honest, kissing you would be like kissing my kid sister." He grimaced.

"You'd think she'd know that. I know you much too well to ever fall in love with you."

"Ditto." He stared out across the brilliant blue surface of the pool. "She's barking up the wrong tree this time. My old man may be loaded, but I'm busted. I don't even have a job and one of these days I'm gonna have to do something about that."

"No problem," Sabrina said, laughing. "She'd give you one. She's after your bloodlines, not your bank account."

He tossed her a cynical glance. "Everybody's after something, I guess." He caught her hand in his and squeezed it as if wanting to assure her full attention, adding seriously, "She's really got a bee in her bonnet about this, Sabrina, in case you didn't know."

"I knew."

"Wonder why?"

She shrugged. "With Lucretia, who can be sure?"

"I've got to admit, the way her mind works sort of…fascinates me."

She gave him a dubious glance. "You gotta be kidding."

"I'm not. When I look at her I can see all those little wheels turning." He made a spiraling gesture with his index finger toward his forehead. "Seriously, she needs to get a life."

"Don't I know it. But it's been years since she showed an interest in any particular man. In the meantime, she's driving me crazy with her machinations. The minute she realizes nothing's afoot with you three, I'm sure she'll come up with another batch of bachelors for my approval, or some other plan that might be even worse."

"Poor Sabrina. Poor little princess." He put one arm around her companionably. "Tell you what, let's keep this little conversation to ourselves. That'll buy you another day or two until the yacht returns to whisk the rejected suitors off the island."

"Why not?" Snuggling into his arm, she gave him a quick kiss on the cheek.

Charley, watching from the veranda, was *not* pleased.

THE YACHT CAME and went and the population of the island dropped to Lucretia, Sabrina, Charley, a full staff of servants and a slew of cowboys nobody ever saw. The two women had walked to the cove to wave goodbye to the trio of rejected suitors, but Charley opted to stay behind and ruminate on the injustices of life, particularly his own.

He hadn't enjoyed seeing Sabrina the target of all that male attention, even after she'd dashed the hopes of the lot of them—not to mention her mother's. For one thing, Charley wasn't all that sure about the Cookie Man, especially after seeing that cozy embrace at the swimming pool.

Now they were gone, and he supposed he wouldn't be far behind. Today was Sabrina's actual birthday, as a matter of fact, so once that was past what was there left to keep him here?

Sabrina's birthday. Suddenly he realized he didn't have a gift for her. Panic filled him; after what she'd given him... With "strangers" in the house, there'd been no chance of her sneaking back into his room...assuming she wanted to. Assuming he'd let her—oh, get a grip! He'd welcome her with open arms.

He commanded himself to stop thinking about her. They'd return to the mainland, Lucretia would realize her little scheme was a bust and they'd all go back to their previous lives.

Would he still get his bonus? He should; if life was fair, he would. But when you were dealing with Lucretia Addison, fair didn't enter into it. He'd definitely made up his mind that the day he got that bonus he was out of there: gone, vanished, out of the lives of the Addison women.

Lucretia charged through the office door, Sabrina on her heels. "Take a memo, Malcolm." Pacing to the window, she looked out across the island. "Call the—"

"Lucretia!" Sabrina was right on her mother's heels. "His name isn't Malcolm!"

Lucretia blinked and frowned. "Of course it's Malcolm. Egads, Bree, this man works with me. I know what to call him."

Sabrina's soft lips curved scornfully; she was on a tear. Charley, trying to catch her eye to warn her off this subject, wondered what had set her off.

"His name," Sabrina said in chilly tones, "is Charley Lawrence."

"He's no *Charley*. It boggles the mind." Lucretia's tone dismissed that notion.

"Too low class?" Sabrina pushed harder.

"No! You're forgetting that *my* other name was Lizzie. You don't get lower class than that." She looked at Charley, who felt like a stick of furniture. "He should be...Matthew, maybe. Or...Clint—sure, Clint would do it."

"Mother!"

Sabrina hadn't called Lucretia that within recent memory and Charley stared.

"Darling!" Lucretia turned to her daughter with outstretched arms. "You called me—"

"I'll call you worse than that if you don't *listen* to me!" Sabrina's smooth cheeks flushed prettily.

"What kind of person doesn't even know the names of her employees? It's disgraceful and...and degrading, that's what it is."

Lucretia cocked her head, her expression suspicious. "What's all this sudden defense of my assistant? I'd say it's none of your business what I call him. If he doesn't mind—"

"How do you know he doesn't? Have you ever asked him? Have you given him a choice?"

"Oh, for—" Lucretia turned on Charley with the majesty of an ocean liner pinning him in its floodlights. "You got a problem with any of this, Malcolm?"

"Who, me?" Charley shrugged and made it a point not to look at Sabrina. She thought she was helping, but she wasn't. "No problems at all, Lucy." Maybe Sabrina would take the hint and pull back.

Maybe she wouldn't. "What do you expect him to say," she flung at her mother, "as long as you sign his paycheck? He can't tell the truth under those circumstances."

"Then I'll fix it so he can," Lucretia said grimly. "Malcolm, you're fired."

"I'm *what?*"

"Fired. Canned. Discharged. Kaput."

"In that case," he said, tossing his leather notebook on the desk, "I'd like to be called 'Charley.'"

Lucretia started to laugh, but Sabrina cut in with a shriek of outrage.

"How dare you!" She marched up to her mother and glared into her eyes, clenched hands extending stiffly at her sides. "Charley's a paragon of virtue and you have the gall to fire him?"

"It doesn't take gall, sweetheart. All it takes is two words—'you're fired.'"

"But you've got no reason!"

"Sabrina," Charley said uneasily, "why don't you just let it go?"

"Because I can't let her get away with this!" Sabrina turned toward him, appealing with her entire body for his support. "She has no reason to treat you this way. Can't we go to the government or something? Isn't this some kind of harassment? I'll bet it's against the law!"

"I've got a reason," Lucretia said grimly. "It's his fault you wouldn't give those three adorable young men a chance. I saw Malcolm or Charley or whoever he is lurking around every corner, watching you—"

"Watching me?" Sabrina looked delighted. "Really?"

"Yes, really. I don't know what he's up to, but I don't intend to let him hang around and cause any more trouble for me, so he's fired, end of debate. As soon as I can contact the yacht I'll send him back to the mainland and out of our lives."

Sabrina whirled toward the dumbfounded man. "If she fires you, I'll hire you! When I offered you a job before, I meant it."

Lucretia turned apoplectic. "Sabrina Addison, you're trying to raid my corporate stable? Of all the nerve!" For a moment Lucretia looked furious, but she managed to harness her temper.

"You fired him. I can hire him."

"Not if I hire him back." Lucretia swung on Charley. "Malcolm, you're rehired."

Charley felt like a Ping-Pong ball. "Maybe I don't

want to work for anyone named Addison, ever again!'' He thrust his hands through his hair in frustration. ''Maybe you're both nuts! Maybe all I want is out of here! Jeez!''

And with that, he turned and strode from the office.

Dumbfounded, Sabrina looked to her mother for guidance. Lucretia raised her eyebrows and shrugged.

''He said 'maybe' we're both nuts,'' she stated. ''We can salvage something from that.'' She put her arm around her daughter's shoulders and Sabrina allowed it. ''There goes the best Malcolm I ever had. Now that I've calmed down a little, I guess I really wouldn't mind hanging on to him.''

''Neither would I,'' Sabrina said in a whisper Lucretia didn't appear to hear.

CHARLEY'S MIND was made up and this time there would be no turning back. Lucretia was crazy and Sabrina was dangerous to his mental health—not to mention his physical health, if her mother ever found out they'd slept together. He was getting out while the getting was good.

If it still was. All through dinner that night, which they both insisted he must share with them, Sabrina kept casting him beseeching glances, while Lucretia treated him as if never had been heard a discouraging word. For his part, *he* treated *them* with a dispassionate courtesy that was hard to maintain, given the circumstances.

As he ruminated over an excellent glass of Cabernet; he realized Lucretia was right, they couldn't work together now. The dynamics had changed in a not-so-subtle way. He no longer thought of himself as a member of the Addison team.

Sabrina's favorite meal was served: caviar, filet mignon, wild rice pilaf and artichoke hearts. The menu merely lent weight to his black mood. The girl had expensive tastes all right. Her birthday cake was a giant cheesecake complete with the kind of fancy curlicues that must have taken some poor baker an entire day to produce. No supermarket special here, declaring a simplistic "Happy birthday, Sabrina" in the sweet, greasy icing he loved.

"Open your gift first," Lucretia demanded, thrusting a jeweler's box across the table. "I had Jordan pick it up for me, so I can vouch for the quality."

One of Sabrina's eyebrows lifted skeptically, but she opened the velvet case. Inside on midnight-blue satin nestled a necklace, if you could call a triple strand of magnificent pink-blushed pearls a "necklace." Charley let out an involuntary whistle.

Sabrina looked at the pearls, too, but her expression never changed. "Thank you," she said, and closed the lid. Then she looked pointedly at Charley.

Who panicked. "H-happy birthday, Sabrina," he said stiffly. "Sorry, I didn't get a chance to shop."

"That's all right, Charley. I didn't expect anything, really."

But she seemed so disappointed that he had to stifle a groan. Reaching into his pocket, he fumbled around desperately, fingers closing around his Swiss Army knife. He hesitated, decided oh, what the hell and drew it forth.

He grimaced, then offered it to her, thinking he must be nuts to embarrass himself publicly this way.

If a triple strand of pearls didn't elicit a squeal of delight, a used pocketknife sure as hell wasn't going to do the trick.

"Here," he said. "I got this for eighth-grade graduation from a social worker who bet me I'd never make it through high school. Fat lot she knew. It's got lots of stuff besides a knife—a corkscrew, a church key—"

"Church key?"

"Bottle opener. And it's got a nail file and tweezers and...happy birthday."

He dropped it into her outstretched hand and she drew it to her, gazing down at it with glowing eyes. "Since the eighth grade! Charley, I'm truly honored. I'll treasure it forever."

A glance at Lucretia showed him that the knife had already been put to use; the woman looked as if it were buried in her heart.

CHARLEY RETIRED early to his room, reluctant to spend a moment more than necessary with the Addison women. Standing on the balcony outside his window, he gazed out over the island and the ocean through thickening fog and tried to figure out how he'd gotten himself into this mess.

Before he could come up with an answer, the moon disappeared behind a cluster of dark clouds. Looking up, Charley realized something was going on here...something with the weather. The wind was coming up and now it howled around the corner of the house, carrying with it a blast of moisture.

"Sir? Sir?"

Glancing around, he saw a member of the house

staff beneath the balcony, the man barely discernible in the fog and darkness.

"What is it?" Charley had to yell above the rush of the wind.

The man cupped his hands around his mouth and shouted back. "Looks like we're about to have a bit of weather. I'd suggest you go back inside and lock those doors and windows tight, pull the shutters closed." With a small salute, he turned and ran across the yard and was soon lost in the dark.

For a moment Charley stood undecided. His instincts were to go back inside, lock up as the man had suggested and crawl into bed. On the other hand, he should do the gentlemanly thing and go in search of the women, to make sure they were all right with this.

Chivalry won. He let himself out into the hall, closed his bedroom door and set off to find the mother and daughter who'd screwed with his life and his head.

He found them in Lucretia's office listening to a weather report on the shortwave radio. When he entered, both glanced up. Lucretia immediately returned her attention to the set, but Sabrina jumped up and ran to his side. Clutching his arm, she looked at him with relief.

"Oh, Charley, I'm glad you came," she breathed. "I was afraid you'd already be in bed asleep."

"Take it easy, Sabrina. Everything will be all right."

She gave him a sheepish smile. "I know you're right, but I've always been afraid of storms. I guess that's because I grew up in California, where the weather never changes. I mean, there's smog or no smog and that's about the extent of it.''

He couldn't resist; he gave her hand a light, comforting squeeze. ''I don't think we're in for much, to tell you the truth.''

''Lot you know about it.'' Lucretia glared at him. She gave the radio a quick blow to its plastic top, but only renewed static greeted her efforts. ''According to the weather reports, we're in for quite a storm.''

''So?'' Charley hiked his brows. ''I've seen rain before, Lucy. I'm sure it'll all be past in time for the yacht to come for me tomorrow. The yacht *is* coming for me tomorrow, isn't it?''

''Now, Malcolm—''

''His name is Charley!'' Sabrina sounded anguished by her failure to impress this upon her mother.

''Charley, Malcolm, what's the big deal?'' Lucretia stood up and glanced around anxiously. ''Did you hear that? Is it the wind or—''

The lights went out.

Sabrina screamed.

Charley whirled toward the sound just as her soft body hurtled against his chest with unerring aim even in the dark. A crash on the other side of the room distracted him; then Lucretia began swearing under her breath.

Charley held Sabrina in his arms, grateful for the winds howling outside the window, which had brought her here. ''Take it easy, everybody,'' he commanded in his best ''don't worry, man in charge'' voice. ''I'm sure the lights will come back on any minute now.''

Lucretia wasn't impressed. Her scornful voice sounded loud and angry in the dark office. "Charley, what the hell do you know about generators? We may be in big trouble here."

"Then let's go find out."

"*I'll* find out. You'd just be in the way. Sabrina?"

"I'm all right," Sabrina responded, her voice a bit muffled against Charley's chest. Somehow she'd managed to find the vee of his shirt collar and her lips brushed his skin when she spoke. "Don't worry about me."

"I *do* worry about you. Charley, you stay here with Sabrina."

"But, Lucy—"

"Will you just do as I say? Bad weather frightens Sabrina, has since she was a little girl. You take care of her while I go see what's going on. I'm sure somebody on the staff is already looking into this."

Charley felt Sabrina's smile against his throat. He swallowed convulsively. "Okay, if you're sure—"

"Of course I'm sure! I'm always sure of everything. I want the two of you to stay right here until I get back. I can't have people wandering around in the dark."

A flashlight beam suddenly sliced through the darkness, accompanied by Lucretia's sigh of relief. "Okay, now we're all right. See you later."

She never even turned the beam around the room, to Charley's relief. If she had, she'd have seen her daughter nestled in her assistant's arms.

They were alone.

"Charley." The soft brush of Sabrina's lips was replaced by a flat-out kiss. "I'm so glad you're here."

"Now, Sabrina, we shouldn't—"

"Why shouldn't we?"

She slid her arms around his waist and snuggled closer. Despite the bravado in her tone, she trembled and he realized she really was frightened. He felt himself weakening.

"Sabrina..."

Something struck the side of the house, the impact reverberating through the darkness. She cried out, her voice filled with panic.

"Easy, sweetheart, easy." Charley patted her on the bottom, realized what he was doing and yanked his hand away. "Must have been a tree limb or something, but it missed the glass. We're all right."

"Are you sure? I'm scared, Charley. It sounds like the end of the world out there."

It did, too; wind howling, rain beating against the glass wall, the timbers of the house creaking and moaning. "It's just noise," he soothed. "It can't hurt us."

"It's hurting me." She shook like a feather in a gale. "If you won't make love to me—"

"Not won't, can't—I mean, don't dare."

"I don't agree, but I can hardly force you. Will you talk to me? Keep me from thinking about how dark and spooky everything is?"

"Sure." Holding her, he edged backward toward a leather sofa that he couldn't see but that he knew was there somewhere. When his legs struck it, he gently drew her down with him until they were seated side by side, his arm protectively around her. "What do you want me to talk about?"

"I don't care. Anything." Something else struck

the house a solid blow and she jumped, her voice rising. "Barbecue. That's something you know a lot about. Tell me about barbecue."

"Barbecue." He'd never been asked to elaborate on his passion before and hardly knew where to start. "Okay. What do you want to know?"

"What's so special about Kansas City barbecue anyway? Isn't barbecue all the same—meat cooked on a grill over charcoal, with a lot of red stuff smeared on it?"

"You're joking, of course." He couldn't believe anybody could be that dumb, even an heiress from Santa Barbara.

"I'm not joking," she said. "Gosh, Charley, you must take your barbecue more seriously than anyone in the world."

That brought forth a sputtering gasp. "Lots of people take it seriously," he protested. "Didn't you ever hear of the Kansas City Barbecue Society? It's made up of folks who take it seriously."

"A whole club for people who like sweating over hot grills?"

He didn't miss the astonishment in her voice. "Hey, why not? They put out a newsletter called the *Bullsheet and*—"

"The bull-*what?*" She giggled.

"You heard me," he growled, pleased that he'd taken her mind off the storm that raged on, unabated. "The slogan of the KCBS is 'It's not just for breakfast anymore!' That should give you some idea about how seriously barbecue is taken."

"What do the members do, sit around and argue about their favorite food?"

"Sometimes. They also analyze it, discuss it, cook it, teach it, write about it, judge it and form posses to look for it. The official purpose is to promote barbecue in any and every way. They also hold contests and publish cookbooks and stuff like that."

"Barbecue contests? How weird." She snuggled closer.

He bristled. "I used to be on a contest team and I can guarantee you, nobody called us 'weird.'"

She surged up to kiss his cheek, managing to press her breasts against his arm in the process. "I'm sorry. Tell me about your team."

"Well," he said, somewhat mollified, "it was me and a big guy called 'Tiny,' who was the chief cook, and as many assistants as he thought we needed. Man, that guy could cook! Ribs, brisket, chicken—Tiny could do it all. Everything I know I learned from him."

"Everything you know about *barbecue.*"

"Yeah, sure. That's what we're talkin'—" He realized she was teasing and added wryly, "You're right. I do take my barbecue seriously."

"That's all right." She patted his cheek. "Tell me more about Tiny."

"Tiny." Charley felt a warm glow just thinking about his old mentor. "Tiny made the greatest sauce in the world—not too sweet, not too hot. And he used nothing but hickory and oak for his fires. He was very particular about the proportions."

"How about mesquite? I knew a guy once who swore by it."

"Texan," Charley said scornfully.

She straightened and twisted toward him, her small hands flat against his chest. "How'd you guess?"

"It wasn't a guess. The biggest regional difference in barbecue is the wood. In Texas, they taint their meat with a lot of mesquite." He felt sufficiently at ease with her to let his scorn show through. "In Oklahoma, they use a lot of hickory and pecan...and *nobody* with any claim to decency uses gas or electric ovens—or charcoal, either, for that matter."

"You're a real purist, Charley Lawrence."

In the darkness, he wasn't prepared for her to move her hand to his thigh, and he jumped about a foot when she did.

"I don't go for MSG, either—monosodium glu-glu-glu—stop that, Sabrina! Get your hands back where they belong."

"You mean *here?*"

"*No!* I mean—" He had to quit talking long enough to catch his breath and corral her roving fingers. When that had been accomplished, he went on a bit breathlessly, "I was telling you about Tiny— I owe that guy a lot. When he picked me up and put me to work, I was just a snot-nosed kid heading for trouble. He gave me something to believe in when I needed it most."

"Is he still...?"

Charley sighed. "He died, but before he did he inspired me to make something out of myself. He also left me his sauce recipe and his dream...to own a barbecue restaurant in Kansas City."

"Darling, isn't that a lot like taking coals to New-castle?"

"What?" Her response completely threw him.

"How many barbecue restaurants do you suppose there already are in Kansas City?"

"I don't know. Seventy, eighty?"

"You don't think that's enough?"

"There's always room for a really good one," he argued. "I've even got the name—Tiny's KCQ."

There was a moment's silence. "I don't get it," she said finally.

"It's a play on words—or letters, or something. We call barbecue 'cue'—*c-u-e*. So I translate that to just the letter *q* and I get KCQ."

"Cute," she said.

He started to laugh. "Sabrina, you don't have a clue what I'm talking about."

"Did you say I don't have a 'cue' or a 'q'?"

"No, I said—"

He reached for her and she playfully pretended to resist him. Within seconds they were wrestling around on the sofa, laughing and gasping for breath and grabbing all kinds of handholds that would never be grabbed in polite company or Olympic competition.

He wasn't prepared for the slash of the flashlight beam; Sabrina's gasp said she wasn't, either.

9

THEY BOLTED to seated attention like two kids caught groping each other in the back seat of a '56 Chevy. With the light in their eyes, Charley couldn't see a thing, but he didn't need to. It was Lucretia.

"Well, well, well," she drawled, keeping them pinned with the beam. "I see you've managed to take my daughter's mind off the weather, Malcolm."

"His name is—"

"Charley. I know what his name is. 'Malcolm' is a compromise until I can come up with something a little more...descriptive. Sabrina, pull down your T-shirt," she added sharply. "You look like you've been wrestling alligators."

Sabrina yanked at her shirt, thrusting out her jaw in that familiar stubborn expression. "It's none of your business who I wrestle, or what."

"As long as you're in my house you will abide by my rules, Miss High and—"

A shaft of lightning seemed to fill every corner of the office with blinding white light, closely followed by a crack of thunder. Sabrina cried out in alarm and Lucretia dropped the flashlight with a strangled oath.

Safe inside the dark again, Charley caught Sabrina's soft hand in his and squeezed. "It's all right," he said, seeking to soothe her. "I'm here. I promise I won't let anything hurt you."

"Oh, Charley," she moaned. "How do you stay so calm with all this going on?"

"It's my job," he said with a grin she couldn't see. "Taking care of you. My boss said I should." He raised his voice to address said boss. "Lucy? Are you all right?"

"I'm fine, but I've dropped the damned flashlight. If I can manage to—"

Before she could finish the thought, she crashed into something that fell with a clatter and the sound of breaking glass. Lucretia began to swear again.

Broken glass added a new and more dangerous element to the proceedings. Charley stood up. "Stay where you are," he told Sabrina. "You, too, Lucretia, and I'll come get you. I got my bearings when the lightning flashed, so I should be able to—"

The huge floor-to-ceiling windows shattered with the impact of some terminal hit. Glass sprayed the room and the roar of the storm intensified. Charley, already on his feet, turned and lunged for the sofa and Sabrina, who burst into tears.

She was lying down, he discovered with relief terrifying in its intensity. The glass couldn't have touched her where she huddled against the back of the sofa. Clinging to her hand, he tried to peer through the darkness.

"Lucretia! Are you all right?"

"I...don't know." Her voice trembled. "I...think so."

"I'll come to get you. Keep talking, but stay where you are."

"Is Sabrina all right?"

"I'm fine, Mother."

"Keep talking, Lucretia."

"What do you want me to say?" Her voice gained strength with every word. "That this damned storm has completely messed everything up? Until we get that generator up and running we won't have electricity or even be able to figure out how much damage this storm has done. Everything that wasn't tied down has been flying around. The cell phone won't work, the radio is out—"

She continued with her litany of complaints while Charley inched toward her in the darkness. Rain slashed through the broken windows, soaking the room and the man who made an upright target as he moved cautiously toward the sound of her voice.

He walked into her outstretched hands, held knee-high to keep from getting stepped on. She was still on the floor, which wasn't good.

"Can you stand up?" he asked, kneeling beside her.

"I...don't know."

He'd never heard her sound so uncertain. Catching her flailing hands, he held them still and called over his shoulder, "You still doing all right, Sabrina?"

"Yes. Don't worry about me, Charley." She sounded in control again—brave, in fact.

"You're doing great," he encouraged her. "Don't be afraid. We'll get out of this all right, but I need you to walk out on your own while I bring your mother. Think you can do that?"

"Of course I can. I'm not afraid when I'm with you."

"That's my girl."

Her soft chuckle reached him. "Don't worry about me," she said. "Help Mother."

Relieved, he leaned over and scooped Lucretia up into his arms. She wasn't trembling; she was as stiff as a board, probably with anger. He tightened his grip and got his feet under him.

"Ready?"

"I was born ready," she grated. "Do your damnedest, Malcolm."

"'Charley,' Mother!" Sabrina's shriek was so close it made him jump. "His name is *Charley,* for heaven's sake!"

"I don't care if his name is Ferdinand the Bull!"

"Shut up and hang on." He rose to his feet, staggering a little. Turning blindly toward where he supposed the inside door must be, he lurched forward with Lucretia in his arms, his feet crunching over glass shards.

CHARLEY TOOK CARE of everything. He got Lucretia settled on a couch in the living room, left Sabrina in charge and went in search of a flashlight Lucretia thought might be in the drawer of her bedside table.

This took a while, and Sabrina found herself growing more and more tense as she waited in the dark beside her mother. Lucretia insisted she wasn't seriously hurt, but Sabrina wasn't sure she believed that. The time seemed to stretch out interminably. After what seemed like a lifetime, they saw the beam of light coming toward them and knew Charley had succeeded in his quest.

Sabrina had never doubted for a second that he

would; he seemed prepared to rise to any occasion. Her admiration for him, already great, increased by the second.

Luckily, Lucretia didn't seem to be seriously injured. She'd suffered a bruise to her left leg, apparently from falling across a small table in the dark. She also had a few nicks and minor cuts from flying glass, as did Charley. Only Sabrina had escaped unscathed, which filled her with an unfamiliar guilt.

"This is all my fault," she wailed. "I should have been the one who suffered. If I had only been more reasonable, none of this—"

Charley and Lucretia yelled "No!" simultaneously.

Lucretia claimed the floor. "Not my beautiful child," she crooned, patting Sabrina's hand and causing Charley, who was bathing the nicks on her shin, to splash water on the carpet. "I'd cut off my right arm before I'd see a hair on your head harmed."

"Th-thank you, Mother," Sabrina said tearfully. She turned a face at once hopeful and contrite toward Charley. "You had something you wanted to say on this subject?"

"I changed my mind." In the shadowy light of the flashlight propped on a nearby table, he looked mysterious and not at all like the Charley she knew. "I've got nothing to say," he reiterated.

Lucretia pushed herself to a sitting position, glowering at him. "You mean you wouldn't take a bullet for my child? Where's your loyalty? What kind of a man *are* you, Malcolm Lawrence?"

"How dare you speak to him that way!" Sabrina matched her mother glare for glare, forgetting the tender emotions she'd been feeling only seconds earlier. "Of course he would—he's a gentleman *and his name is Charley!*"

"Don't shout at me, Sabrina Addison. I'm still your mother and I deserve a little respect."

"Everybody deserves respect," Sabrina declared piously, "including—" She looked around, startled to discover that the man for whom she was doing battle was exiting the room without a word, without a light, without bothering even to say goodbye.

Darn! She'd had interesting plans for him and now she was stuck with her mother. She added a petulant, "Now see what you've done. He's gone."

"See what *I've* done? Dear heart, he's quite accustomed to me and my little...peculiarities. It's you flinging flies in the ointment."

"Ugh! What a revolting remark."

"Nevertheless, I'm right as usual." Sighing, Lucretia relaxed back on the arm of the couch. "I must admit, I'm glad he's gone. He was quite helpful in a crisis, but the storm is dying down now and we don't need him any longer."

"Maybe *you* don't need him, but I've got a different take on it."

"Oh, Lord!" Lucretia eyed her daughter askance. "Don't tell me—"

"Then I won't."

"Yes, you will! I insist."

"In that case..." Sabrina drew the words out deliberately. "At first I thought what I felt for Charley was simply admiration. You know, for the way he's put up with us since we've been on this godforsaken island. Then he took charge and practically saved our lives when the window blew."

"Oh, good. That's fine. Admiration is certainly an acceptable response." Lucretia patted her daughter's hand. "If you'll just help me up, I'll—"

"*But then* I realized that what I feel is much more than admiration. Just this very moment I realize that what I feel for Charley Lawrence is—"

"Don't say it! Please don't." Lucretia covered her eyes with a bent arm.

Sabrina said it with relish. "Love! What I feel for Charley Lawrence is *love*, Mother, whether you like it or not."

Only later, much later, did Sabrina, who rarely succumbed to hindsight, wonder if she'd said that because it was true or just to bug her mother—which would make her just as shallow as Charley thought she was.

BECAUSE OF the excitement the night before, Charley slept later than usual the next morning, not even stirring until almost nine. For a few moments he lay in bed wondering why he felt so tired and depressed, then remembered and wished he hadn't. To hell with soul-searching, he decided. The sooner he got off this damned island the better.

The first thing he did was pack. He had no idea when the yacht would appear but when it did, he'd be ready. He no longer had any reason to stay. The electrical power had been restored while he slept, the house was functioning, the women had survived their ordeal without too much damage and last but not least, Charley no longer had a job that required him to kowtow to a crazy person.

By the time he walked into the dining room he'd worked himself into what one of his many foster mothers used to call "a real tizzy." Habit came to his rescue, however, and he greeted Lucretia and Sabrina with cool disinterest, feigned but, he was sure, convincing.

The Addison women sat at the long, shiny table, one at one end and one at the other. Neither looked especially perky, and he noticed that Sabrina had dark circles beneath her beautiful eyes.

He walked over to the sideboard, poured himself a cup of coffee and surveyed the battleground. Where to sit without choosing sides? Counting the number of chairs, he chose number three, smack-dab in the middle.

"So," Lucretia said, stirring sugar into her coffee, "did you get any sleep at all last night, Mal—Char—Assistant?"

"I'm no longer your assistant, and yes, I slept quite well, thank you." Heaven would forgive him the lie.

"I didn't," Sabrina said with a sigh.

She looked quite tragically lovely, sitting there with that glorious hair streaming over her shoulders. Dressed all in white, she looked cool and ethereal.

"Charley, you saved our lives last night."

"That's an enormous exaggeration, Sabrina, but I know better than to argue with you." He poured coffee into his cup from the silver carafe.

"Good." She stared down at a slice of toast on a plate before her. "Are you angry with me?"

He'd never heard her sound so uncertain. Actually,

he'd never heard her sound uncertain to any discernible degree, period. "Of course not," he said, angry with himself because she made him question his own emotions and then lie about them.

She looked up and her gaze caught his. "Then you'll stay on the island until we can all leave together? Lucretia says we have to make an inventory of the damage first so we can send out repairmen and replace everything that was broken."

"It's out of the question." The coffee was bitter. He drank it anyway.

"But—"

"Sabrina, I don't have a job, which means I don't have a reason to be here. I'm throwing good time after bad at this point."

Lucretia leaned forward, striking the shiny tabletop with the flat of her hand. "I rehired you. What are you carrying on about now?"

"I didn't accept your kind offer," he said sarcastically. "Would you be so good as to tell me what time to expect the yacht?"

She glanced at a diamond-encrusted wristwatch. "Any time now, actually." Her expression, her very face, had turned cold and unyielding.

"Mother," Sabrina demanded, "you've got to make him stay."

"I can't make him stay." Lucretia's tone left no doubt that she not only couldn't, she didn't want to.

"But—" Sabrina turned beseechingly to Charley. "I can't let you just...just go out of my life this way. We've been through too much together."

"It's for the best," he said, still cool, wishing his stomach hadn't clenched into a knot of denial. *For-*

ever was a very long time indeed. "If you'll excuse me—" He started to rise.

"You haven't eaten."

"I don't seem to have much of an appetite."

"Mother, do something!"

Charley was halfway to the door, when he heard Lucretia's response.

"He had his chance. It's out of my hands."

"But—"

He didn't wait to hear Sabrina's response, just went upstairs to get his gear before heading down to the wharf. This was one boat he did not intend to miss.

"CHARLEY, WAIT for me!"

He walked faster.

"Charley!"

Sabrina's frustration was so penetrating that he finally halted on the trail in spite of himself. Hoisting his small bag from one hand to the other, he waited for her to catch up.

She was graceful even on the unpaved pathway—a shortcut to the cove. Panting, she smiled up at him.

"The least I can do is see you off," she gasped.

"Not necessary," he said shortly. "Go on back to the house, why don't you?"

"Not a chance." She slipped one hand beneath his elbow and turned back down the path. "Is that all the luggage you've got?"

"No, but some cowboy on a horse took the other bag down." This wasn't working; the path wasn't broad enough for them to walk abreast, and drop-offs of various depths threatened on both sides. He steered her ahead of him.

She glanced back. "Things got pretty battered last
night. Lots of trees uprooted and even a few buildings
knocked down." She added almost hopefully, "Do
you suppose it was a tornado?"

"Not even close." He'd been in one of those once
and spoke with authority. "Sabrina, you're just making everything harder. Why are you doing this?"

She glanced back again and stumbled. He caught
her elbows until she'd regained her balance, thinking
that if she tumbled off the trail she could really be
hurt. That thought made him feel slightly ill.

"I don't want you to go," she said miserably. "Lucretia's being a total bitch about this. I may never
speak to her again."

"Sure you will." He sighed and dropped the bag.
"It's time for me to go, maybe past time. I've got my
own life to worry about and—"

"Hoo-hoo! Malcolm! Sabrina? Hoo-hoo!"

Lucretia stood at the top of the rise behind them,
waving frantically. "Wait for me!" She started forward at a reckless pace. "I've got something to tell—
oops!"

And she tripped and toppled off the trail and out
of sight, whether into a ravine or all the way to the
beach below impossible to tell.

Sabrina screamed. "Oh, my God, she's fallen!
We've got to help her!"

"I'll do it. You wait here and stay out of trouble."
Charley leaped up the trail, his heart pounding before
he took the first step. Lucretia might be trouble with
a capital *T*, but the thought of her broken body lying
at the foot of the cliff filled him with cold terror.

He topped the rise and turned sharply in the direc-

tion she'd disappeared. Plunging past a clump of
bushes, he stopped short. There on a small ledge no
more than six feet below the level of the trail sat
Lucretia Addison, leaning back on arms propped behind her.

She glared up at him as if it were *his* fault she was
in such a mess. "Well?" she demanded. "What are
you waiting for? Get me out of here!"

"Damnation, Lucy!" He cast about for the best
way to get down to her. "Maybe I should just leave
you where you are until I can get the hell off this
island."

Sabrina reached his side just in time to hear that
remark. "Don't be ridiculous," she said, as if he'd
been serious. "You'd never do such a thing." Peering
over the edge, she called, "Mother, are you all
right?"

"Of course I am. Clumsiness isn't usually terminal—ow!" Lucretia paused in the act of rising, bend-
ing forward to rub her leg. It was the same leg she'd
bruised the previous evening. "My pants are caught
on some horrible bush." She began to tug at the recalcitrant fabric.

"Hold on," Charley ordered. "I'll be right down."

"Maybe...you'd better," she agreed. White lines
of strain bracketed her mouth.

Charley picked his spot, then leaped lightly down
beside her. "What was so all-fired important that you
had to throw caution to the wind and come charging
down the hill that way?" he demanded.

"It seemed important at the time, but—Malcolm,
be careful!"

"I am being careful." He yanked on her pant leg

and found it well and truly impaled by the bush. Groping around in his pocket, he groaned.

His handy dandy Swiss Army knife was gone. Instinctively, he glanced up at Sabrina. Something came hurtling toward him and he reached out and grabbed his knife from midair.

"I'm never without it," she called down to him. "Since the day you gave it to me, Charley...."

A warm feeling of approval swept over him. Working quickly, he cut the pant leg free, pocketed the knife and picked Lucretia up in his arms. Casting about, he spotted an easier, but longer, ascent to the main trail and headed for it.

She refused to put her arm around his shoulder or cling in any fashion. Instead, she crossed her arms over her chest and glared straight ahead. "I remember what was so all-fired important," she announced stiffly. "The yacht's not coming today."

"What?" Charley tossed her into the air a couple of inches for emphasis, catching her when she came down again.

The fright broke through her reserve and she grabbed his neck and hung on. "Don't yell at me!" she yelled at him. "And don't you drop me, either, if you know what's good for you."

"Threats? What the hell else can you *do* to me?" he asked rhetorically. The path he followed wasn't too steep but it was circuitous. Climbing it with a woman in his arms could definitely be classified as work. "You've humiliated me, insulted me and fired me more times than I can count. You have, in short... made a fool of...me and..."

"Shut up, Charley," she grated. "You can't carry me up a mountain and talk at the same time."

"Aha!" cried Sabrina, watching their progress from the path above. "You do know his name!"

"Of course I do. I'm not a total idiot. But I have a right to call my employees anything I choose to call them, and all my assistants are called 'Malcolm.' It's part of the job description."

"Oh, Mother!"

"Oh, Sabrina!"

"Oh, hell."

"ALL RIGHT, LUCRETIA, tell me what the deal is with that boat."

Lucretia reclined with a groan on the cushions of the couch in the living room, exactly where she'd been the night before. Sabrina, positioning a pillow beneath her left knee, paused to listen.

"That's what I was trying to tell you," Lucretia said in a cranky tone. "I got a call this morning right after you left, saying the yacht had developed some kind of... I don't know, some kind of mechanical problem. It'll be delayed at least twenty-four hours, maybe more."

"Well, I'll be a son of a—" Charley bit off the curse already picked out and eager to be said. He wouldn't give her the satisfaction. "I don't believe you, of course."

"Of all the nerve! I've *never* lied to you."

"You've never told me the truth. You are the most conniving, manipulating, underhanded—"

"Charley," Sabrina cut in anxiously, "remember that's my mother you're talking about."

He stared at her. "That's nothing to what *you've* said about her."

"She's my mother, so I can. But I really wish *you* wouldn't." She gave him a luminous smile. "You're the one who advised me to give her the benefit of the doubt. You're the one who talked about her charm. You're the one who—"

"Okay, okay, you don't have to throw every stupid thing I've ever said back in my face."

"I'd never do that. The only truly stupid thing you ever said was 'I'm leaving.' Don't you want to take that back?"

"No!" He was distracted by Lucretia's groan and he turned to her. "Is there anything you need before I try to figure out a way to get off this…island?"

"A good doctor and a shot of brandy," she retorted. "I'm in agony. I think my leg is broken. Maybe in two or three places."

Sabrina bent over the afflicted appendage, frowning anxiously. "Don't be ridiculous," she said bravely. "I'm sure it's nothing more than a sprain."

Lucretia groaned again, more dramatically. "Who *are* you and what have you done with my daughter?" she demanded. "My daughter gets hysterical at the first hint of a crisis and you're acting like Dr. Ruth and telling me I'm fine, when I know I'm incapacitated for life."

Sabrina burst out laughing. "Dr. Ruth is a sex therapist."

"Leave it to you to know *that,*" Lucretia said darkly. "Do I get my brandy or do I just have to lie here and suffer?"

Charley backed away. "You two handle this. I've got some thinking to do."

Sabrina started forward anxiously. "Wait, I'll go with you and we can—"

"I want to go alone," he said sharply. "I'm really ticked off and there are only two ways to get over it. One is solitude."

"And the other is…?" Sabrina eyed him hopefully.

Yeah, that, too, he thought. But what he said was, "The other is to throw a big chunk of meat on the barbecue and drink beer until it's finished. Since that's out of the question—"

"Why is it out of the question?"

Both Charley and Sabrina, caught up in their own conversation, looked blankly at Lucretia, installed like a queen on her throne.

"Well, because…what would I cook?" Charley asked rhetorically. "What kind of wood—"

"You'd cook any damned thing we've got in the freezer or on the hoof on this island. As for wood, we've got a ton of it tossed all over the place like so many matchsticks. If you're too good to pick it up yourself—"

"I'll do it!" Sabrina cried. "Please, Charley, let me gather wood for you."

Damn, just the thought of doing his thing barbecue-wise filled him with an anticipation he frankly hadn't anticipated. It wouldn't be the same, of course. He wouldn't have the kind of wood he preferred, or the right kind of grill, and probably not even all the spices and condiments he needed. But at least he could take a stab at it, which would take his mind off his current horrible predicament: stranded on an island with a woman he couldn't resist...and her mother.

He realized both women were staring at him, the older with a kind of double-dare-you expression and the younger with the eager faith of the untried.

"Sure," he said, because he was weak—*weak*. "Why not? Sabrina, you can be my assistant. It won't be the real thing—"

"Real what thing?" Lucretia wanted to know.

"Mother!" Sabrina glared. "Kansas City barbecue, what else?"

"What else, indeed?" Lucretia rolled her eyes toward the ceiling. "It'll be close enough for government work, as they say. Just hand me the cell phone and then you two can run along. I'll just lie here and suffer."

Somehow Charley got the feeling she was shocked when they did that very thing.

THE COOK WAS more than happy to relinquish her kitchen to Charley's care. When assured she wouldn't be needed until the following day, she whisked off her snowy apron, tossed it on a counter and took off for her own home, shared with her cowboy husband.

Looking around the gleaming expanse, Charley felt as if he'd died and gone to heaven. It was a gorgeous kitchen, all chrome and stainless steel, with restaurant-style stove and refrigerator and a walk-in freezer. On a patio off the kitchen stood a huge smoker-barbecue, which probably hadn't been used twice since it was installed.

He felt his mood lightening by the minute. This was exactly what he needed. He just had to make sure he didn't allow it to soften his mood toward the Addison women, especially the gorgeous one looking at him with big, brown, adoring eyes.

10

"So," LUCRETIA SAID suspiciously, looking down at the overflowing bounty on her plate, "this is genuine Kansas City barbecue, is it?"

"No," Charley corrected her with considerable annoyance, "this is genuine Addison Island barbecue. I couldn't do the real thing with what I've got available here. Hell, I used wood I've never even *seen* before. And the sauce is close, but not quite the real thing."

Sabrina leaned forward eagerly, resting her forearms on the gleaming wood of the table. "He has a secret recipe, Mother."

"He does, does he?" Lucretia cocked her head and gave him a cynical look. "What's in it that makes it so secret?"

Charley laughed. "If I told you, it wouldn't be a secret, would it?" He picked up his napkin and dropped it in his lap. "It's put-up-or-shut-up time, folks. But I want the truth, you both got that? If you don't like it, don't try to spare my feelings."

Impatiently he watched them consider plates brimming with ribs and chicken and coleslaw. Lucretia picked up her fork and poked tentatively at a rib.

"Not that way!" He grabbed a rib with his fingers. "You pick it up like this—and you take a big bite."

It wasn't bad. It wasn't great, but it wasn't bad. "Then you have a drink of beer."

He reached for the can, which looked completely out of place at the elegant table, and took a big swig. "Ahh." He sighed with pleasure. "Can't eat 'cue without beer. That's why barbecuers' hands are permanently curved."

Dutifully Sabrina followed his instructions, as did Lucretia, but with less enthusiasm. Charley could understand why; her fingers, with their long, curved nails and diamond rings, looked curiously misplaced on a crusty, brown rib.

"Charley!" Sabrina licked her lips, her eyes wide with admiration. "This is wonderful."

He'd expected her to say that, but was nonetheless pleased. Lucretia, however, was going to tell the truth filtered through whatever her secret agenda might be at the moment. She wasn't going to like it, though. There was nothing to be gained by enthusiasm and Lucretia always had *something* to gain or she didn't play.

He watched with rabid attention while she picked up a rib and held it daintily to her lips for a nibble. She chewed thoughtfully, then bravely tried another, following it with a sip of beer. She tapped her linen napkin against her mouth.

"Well?"

"I have to be honest," she said.

"I guess you do," he agreed, disappointed. At least Sabrina seemed to like it. "Hit me with your best shot. I'm tough. I can take it."

"Dear Malcolm—"

" 'Charley'!"

"Thank you, darling. Charley, I'm no expert on barbecue—"

"This is hardly news."

"Don't be testy." She lowered her brows in warning. "You may not work for me any longer, but—"

"Lucretia, do you like the damn rib or don't you?"

"I love it," she said serenely, dabbing her fingers on the napkin before dropping it in her lap and reaching for the rib again. "This is beyond a doubt the best barbecue I've ever tasted. You're a master chef, Charles. You are to be commended."

And while he watched in astonishment, she attacked the rib with relish.

"CHARLEY! CHARLEY, are you awake?"

A patting on the door accompanied Sabrina's softly urgent call. Dinner, a stunningly successful affair, was long over. Standing just outside his bathroom door with a toothbrush in his mouth, Charley groaned.

He wasn't up to this tonight. Knowing that tomorrow he'd be sailing out of her life forever, he didn't need any more memories of what he couldn't have.

Walking close to the door, he called out a sudsy, "Go away!"

The door promptly opened and Sabrina walked inside. "Thanks for the invitation," she said cheerfully. She didn't seem surprised to see him standing there in khaki shorts and nothing else, a toothbrush in his mouth.

He removed the impediment to clear speech. "I said go away, not come in."

"You know, it's a funny thing, but when it's mumbled around a toothbrush it sounds the same."

She strolled across the room and sat down on the

foot of his bed. She had on some filmy white thing with a bunch of layers that changed the view with every move she made. Although she seemed perfectly at ease, he wasn't.

She smiled and waved toward the open bathroom door. "Maybe you'd like to lose the toothbrush before we talk."

"Who says we're going to talk?" That was simply bravado, of course. He went into the bathroom and rinsed the suds out of his mouth before returning to face his worse nightmare: Sabrina, warm and willing, and completely beyond his reach.

"So what's the problem now?" he asked brusquely.

With a tapered forefinger, she traced a golden whorl in the brocaded bedspread. "What makes you think I've got a problem?"

"Because there's no other reason for you to be here."

"You don't think so?"

She looked up at him suddenly and he saw to his horror that tears welled in her velvet eyes. Automatically he took a step toward her, all his resolve melting away. "Ah, Sabrina..."

"No, don't worry about me." She shook her head, bravely, he thought. "I...I'm only here because I'm so worried about you, Charley." She punctuated her words with a little sob.

"Me? Why?" He edged closer to the bed.

"Because you're a genius—you really are." Her voice rang with sincerity. "You've got to be the best barbecuer in...in the world!"

"Well, maybe not the world," he objected modestly. "But I'm in the top two in Kansas City maybe—which now that I think of it is the world according to barbecue.''

"That's right!'' She patted the bed beside her and kept on talking. "To think that your dream will be dashed because of me is more than I can bear.''

He was seated beside her before he knew what he was doing. "It's not your fault, Sabrina. I guess it wasn't meant to be.''

She turned to him, her hands clasped between her breasts. The effect of that was to tighten that filmy stuff to reveal her nipples, twin peaks of temptation. "I can't believe that's true.'' She seemed to sway toward him, as if propelled by the force of that belief. "You deserve…everything…you want.'' She licked her luscious pink lips. "Everything…''

"I—you—we—''

"Yes, darling. That, too.'' She unclasped her hands and transferred them to his naked chest so smoothly it seemed preordained. "If there's anything I can say…or do…to convince you that your dreams are as important to me as they are to you…''

He dragged in a deep, shuddering breath. Her beautiful face was so close that he could see clearly the fine texture of her skin, the amazing length of her curving eyelashes. "There might be something,'' he croaked.

"Name it,'' she whispered. "If it's mine to give…''

It was. And she did.

SABRINA SIMPLY KNOCKED his socks off, or would have had he been wearing any. It dawned on Charley slowly that he'd been had. *Very* slowly, actually...after he and Sabrina had spent considerable time mostly horizontal.

He'd never encountered a woman so giving, or a woman with so much to give. Nor had he ever encountered a woman—besides Lucretia—who was so sure of what she wanted and willing to go after it.

Thus it was that he found himself lying flat on his back next to her in a tornado-struck bed, completely satisfied and trying desperately to generate a little righteous indignation around him. He couldn't believe he'd let her do this to him again.

He couldn't imagine why she'd wanted to. Talk about the princess and the commoner...

She snuggled against him, one hand roving over his chest and stomach. She sighed blissfully.

He wondered what she would say now, to further confuse the issue. She was going to make things worse no matter what words came out of her mouth. They were strangers in the night, so to speak; he'd go his way and she'd go hers.

She'd probably never think of him again, but he knew he'd think about her plenty. Hell, he loved her. It was going to take more than mileage to get her out of his system...and his heart.

"Charley," she whispered, tickling his belly button with a fingernail. "Are you awake?"

He shuddered. *Was* he awake? "Yeah," he growled. "What's on your mind?"

"Nothing much, I just...wondered if you're going to marry me now."

Oh, cute. That was just what he needed, her making jokes. "Yeah, right. Lucretia can be matron of honor." He captured her roving hand and held it still, adding, "You getting your jollies here, Sabrina? Because none of this strikes me as too damn funny."

She kissed his chest. "I didn't mean it to be funny," she murmured. "I'm dead serious. Will you marry me, Charley Lawrence?"

"I—will I—are you— Shit!" Charley jerked away from her, rolled over and sat up on the edge of the bed. Shoving his tousled hair out of his face with both hands, he leaned his elbows on his knees and tried desperately to think.

"Is that a yes or a no?" Sliding up behind him, she pressed her lips to the small of his back.

He flinched as if prodded with a spear but couldn't bring himself to bound from the bed as he knew he should. "It's a no," he croaked. "*N-o,* no...."

She kissed her way around his waist. "Oh, come on," she teased. "Tell me how you really feel? It's a great idea. What's wrong with it?"

"Other than the fact that it's impossible?"

"Why impossible?" She came up beneath his arm and smiled up at him.

"Let me count the ways." Which would have been easier without her draped across his naked lap. "In the first place, I could never marry a woman with your money and prospects...and mother."

"Why not? A smart guy like you should be able to see the advantages."

She moved constantly in a variety of interesting ways. He could hardly breathe. He caught his breath sharply, waited until he could speak coherently again before replying. "And what might these alleged advantages be?"

"You know, Charley. You're the one who told

me.'' She found an unkissed spot on his anatomy and proceeded to correct that oversight.

Charley's head was spinning and his flesh burned for her. "Refresh my memory," he groaned.

"Well..." Slight hesitation while she kissed everything else she could reach, quite thoroughly. "As you said to me not long ago, you'd be crazy to look love and good fortune in the mouth." It was a gentle reminder.

"You know how you throw my own words back at me? I hate when that happens." He shifted slightly, spreading his legs. Before she could do anything about that, he caught her beneath the arms and lifted, dragged her around and lowered her until she was astride his thighs.

She chewed on her bottom lip, settling herself with exquisite care. "Charley, darling, you taught me a lot about dealing with the cantankerous people you love. Remember what you said? 'She may show her love in inappropriate ways, but so what?' You were talking about my mother but it applies here, too. Darling, I may show *my* love in inappropriate ways, but so what? That's part of my charm."

Inappropriate ways? This woman hadn't done an inappropriate thing in her life as far as Charley Lawrence was concerned. Right up to and including now, when she moved against him, her breathing accelerating along with his.

And then a new and wondrous realization sank in. "Love? You love me?"

She sighed, arching her back. "With all my heart. But..." She began to move more quickly. "You loved me first, of course."

"Of course." At the moment he'd have admitted

to just about anything to keep her keeping on. In this
case, however, it happened to be the truth. He slid his
hands under her bare bottom and lifted.

"The question is," she gasped, "do you love me
enough to modify your dream...just slightly...
because I *really* don't want to live in Kansas City."

"Where's Kansas City?"

TOGETHER THEY WENT to confront the dragon. They
found her stretched out on the couch in the living
room, her leg on a cushion and a telephone in hand.
When she saw them enter together, she grimaced.

When she noticed Sabrina's hand enfolded in Charley's, she hung up the telephone none too gently.

"Well, Malcolm," she said curtly, "why are you
still here?"

"Because your damn boat didn't come."

"And don't call him 'Malcolm'!"

"If he doesn't mind, why should you?"

"I mind!"

Both women looked at Charley in mutual astonishment.

Lucretia recovered first. "You yelled at me," she
accused. "You can't yell at me. I'm your boss."

"Not anymore, you're not." Feeling the last ves-
tiges of Lucretia's control over his life lifting like a
gossamer veil, Charley advanced upon her. "My
name is Charles Lawrence, as you well know. Use
it."

"Oh, good Lord." Lucretia rolled her eyes as if
she couldn't believe this. "If you truly intend to leave
my employ, I don't see what difference it makes

whether I call you 'Malcolm' or 'Charles' or 'Spot the Dog.'"

Sabrina clung to Charley, gazing up at him adoringly. "It makes a lot of difference," she said, "because—"

"Let me tell her," Charley said grimly. "Lucy, we—"

"I'm not sure I want to hear this," Lucretia said, dramatically covering her eyes with her arm. "I'm not up to bad news. Why don't you just run along and we'll forget the whole thing?"

"Not a chance," Charley said. He felt light-headed with relief; there was nothing she could do to hurt him. Sabrina loved him. All he wanted from Lucretia was to be left alone. "Lucretia," he went on in a firm tone, "I'm going to marry your daughter."

For the longest time, Lucretia lay there quivering like a tuning fork. Then she slowly uncovered her eyes. "You proposed to Sabrina?"

"No, Mother, I proposed to him," Sabrina said proudly. "He finally said yes."

"Why?" Lucretia wondered aloud.

"Because we love each other!" Charley and Sabrina said fervently, in unison.

Charley added, "We're sorry if you don't like it, but that's the way it is."

Sabrina leaned forward, her firm little chin thrust out at a pugnacious angle. "Don't try to change my mind, Mother," she warned. "You've been after me for years to get married. Now that I'm ready to do it, don't think I'm going to let you or anybody else come between me and the man I love. I know he's not the country-club type you seem to favor, but he's the man I want. And he's mine. All mine."

Lucretia's very lack of response was making Charley nervous. Screams and threats and tantrums he could handle, but not this stillness. "I'll spend the rest of my life trying to make Sabrina happy," he ventured. "In case you're worried that I'm a fortune hunter—"

"Charley!" Sabrina stared at him.

"No, this is important," he persisted. "In case you think I'm a fortune hunter, Lucretia, I want you to know that I'm going to insist on a prenuptial agreement. The only thing Sabrina's got that I want is herself."

Sabrina snuggled closer in his arms. "Charley, that's so sweet."

"Yeah, well—" He kept his attention on his beloved's mother.

Who finally sat up, swinging her sore leg around until her feet rested on the floor. "You two really love each other?" she asked with icy control.

"Yes!"

She sucked in a deep, quick breath. "In that case, Charles, I'm offering you a vice presidency at Addison Enterprises."

"You're *what?*" He stared at her with horror. Slip back into that web on purpose? "Not a chance!"

"Not a chance!" Sabrina echoed.

Lucretia's voice dropped to a purr. "Even if we're talking about vice president of Addison's new restaurant project?"

Charley flinched. "What new restaurant project? I don't know anything about any restaurant project."

"That's because it's brand-new," Lucretia said. "The only holdup has been finding the right man to head it. It's quite obvious that man is you."

"Serve at the pleasure of my mother-in-law? No way."

"Even if we're talking a chain of *barbecue* restaurants?" Lucretia peered at the stunned couple from beneath lowered lashes.

Sabrina gasped and threw her arms around Charley's neck. "Darling! It's your dream come true!"

"Not exactly." He held her away from him just enough so he could see her face. "You're the one who's been telling me that we can't trust your mother. Now you're saying I should take her up on her phony offer?"

"I don't think it's phony." She glanced at Lucretia. "Is it?"

"Not at all." Lucretia looked properly incensed at the very idea. "I *have* been thinking about a new restaurant chain. I'll admit, until I tasted barbecue à la Charles, that aspect never occurred to me. Now it seems obvious."

Sabrina returned her attention to Charley. "See? She means it. Darling." She placed her soft hands on either side of his face. "You'd be crazy to look Lucretia's money and generosity in the mouth."

"Are you going to hit me with that every time we disagree?" he demanded.

"Of course not. Just when it's appropriate. Charley, Lucretia loves me and I love you. Why shouldn't she give you the consideration you so richly deserve?"

Lucretia leaned forward. "I thought we could call the chain KCQ—Kansas City 'Cue. That's what you 'in' guys call barbecue, right?"

"Who told you that?" Charley demanded suspiciously. "I don't think I did. Did I?"

"A little bird told me," Lucretia said impatiently. "What difference does it make? Charles, I'm offering you the chance of a lifetime. But I won't beg. I've got too much pride for that. If you want to go to Sabrina with nothing—no job, no prospects, no nothin'—that's up to you. But if you'll take a word of advice—"

A word of advice? Lucretia didn't come up with words of advice; she came up with schemes and plots and machinations that would impress Machiavelli. If he thought she was the boss from hell and the mother from hell, how would she stack up as a mother-in-law?

It was a damn good thing he loved Sabrina to distraction, because everything in him screamed *run.*

He swallowed hard. "Okay, Lucy. What words of advice do you have for me?"

"Take the girl and the job and all the little goodies life is about to throw at you and stop looking this particular gift horse in the mouth. That's my advice to you, dear boy."

Both women waited for his response. Charley sighed.

"Yeah," he said at last, "you're right. What could be more appropriate than knighting the commoner so he'll be good enough to marry the princess?"

"May I take that as a yes?" Lucretia pressed relentlessly.

"It's a yes." Charley surrendered to the newest incarnation of his dream. "Assuming you're willing to make that *Tiny's* KCQ."

Only later…much later…did Charley and Sabrina ponder: had Lucretia planned the whole thing…or not?

Epilogue

"TAKE A MEMO, Malcolm."

Lucretia Addison swung toward her new assistant, hired only a couple of days ago as the latest in a long line of potential replacements for the now vice president in charge of Addison's newest venture, Tiny's Genuine KCQ restaurant chain.

Brigg Newton, known to his cantankerous boss since childhood, grimaced. Lucretia knew his name, but for some reason insisted on calling him "Malcolm." Charley had warned his latest replacement that would happen, and advised that if it presented a problem, it should be nipped in the bud right away.

Brigg hadn't bothered, figuring, what the hell? It was all in a day's work.

Actually, Charley had advised against taking the job at all, but beggars couldn't be choosers. It was work or welfare for Brigg Newton and he figured working for Lucretia Addison was a step up from his last job: lifeguard at his father's country club.

So he picked up his leather-bound notebook and waited for further instructions.

"This is my to-do list for today," she announced.

"First, I want my people in Tokyo to proceed with the acquisition of that computer company we've been dancing around with for so long."

"You got it, Lucy." Brigg wrote, then waited for item number two.

"Second..." Lucretia paced to the glass wall and stared out at the city of Los Angeles, at her feet where it belonged. "I saw a Bentley in a showroom on my way to work this morning. I want it here by the close of business today."

"A little fast, but I'll do my best." Brigg wrote it down.

"No, dear boy, you don't understand. The car's here by the end of the day or it's no sale."

"I'll be sure to mention that." He stifled a smile. Lucretia Addison cracked him up. She was so friggin' sure about *everything*. He wondered idly what it'd be like to see her thrown into a situation where she wasn't the queen bee.

"And last but not least..."

"Name it and it's yours," Brigg assured her, thinking, *This job is going to be fun.*

"Last but not least—" she whirled to face him, determination etched on her face *"—I want a grandchild!"*

Brigg felt his own face blanch. "I'm not sure that's something I have any say about," he hedged.

"Shut up and listen," she blazed at him. "I want a grandchild, and since that means dealing with my darling daughter and my incredibly stubborn son-in-law, that's where you, dear Malcolm, come in...."

Jeez, Brigg thought, listening with awe while she laid out her plan. The matchmaking mother from hell was turning into the wannabe grandmother from hell right before his eyes.

Lots of luck, Charley and Bree, he thought. *You're sure as hell gonna need it!*

Happy Birthday to

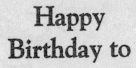

It's party time....
This year is our
40th anniversary!

**Forty years of
bringing you the best
in romance fiction—and
the best just keeps
getting better!**

To celebrate, we're planning
three months of fun, and prizes.

Not to mention, of course,
some fabulous books...

The party starts in **April** with:

Betty Neels
Emma Richmond
Kate Denton
Barbara McMahon

Come join the party!

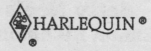

By the bestselling author of *FORBIDDEN FRUIT*

FORTUNE

ERICA SPINDLER

Be careful what you wish for...

Skye Dearborn knew exactly what to wish for. To
unlock the secrets of her past. To be reunited with her
mother. To force the man who betrayed her to pay.
To be loved.

One man could make it all happen. But will Skye's
new life prove to be all that she dreamed of...or a
nightmare she can't escape?

Be careful what you wish for...it may just come true.

Available in March 1997 at your favorite retail outlet.

MIRA The brightest star in women's fiction

As Seen on TV!

Free Gift Offer

With a Free Gift proof-of-purchase
from any Harlequin® book, you can receive
a beautiful cubic zirconia pendant.

This stunning marquise-shaped stone is a genuine cubic
zirconia—accented by an 18" gold tone necklace.
(Approximate retail value $19.95)

Send for yours today...
compliments of ⬧HARLEQUIN®

To receive your free gift, a cubic zirconia pendant, send us one original proof-of-purchase, photocopies not accepted, from the back of any Harlequin Romance®, Harlequin Presents®, Harlequin Temptation®, Harlequin Superromance®, Harlequin Intrigue®, Harlequin American Romance®, or Harlequin Historicals® title available in February, March or April at your favorite retail outlet, together with the Free Gift Certificate, plus a check or money order for $1.65 U.S./$2.15 CAN. (do not send cash) to cover postage and handling, payable to Harlequin Free Gift Offer. We will send you the specified gift. Allow 6 to 8 weeks for delivery. Offer good until April 30, 1997, or while quantities last. Offer valid in the U.S. and Canada only.

Free Gift Certificate

Name: _____

Address: _____

City: _____ State/Province: _____ Zip/Postal Code: _____

Mail this certificate, one proof-of-purchase and a check or money order for postage and handling to: HARLEQUIN FREE GIFT OFFER 1997. In the U.S.: 3010 Walden Avenue, P.O. Box 9071, Buffalo NY 14269-9057. In Canada: P.O. Box 604, Fort Erie, Ontario L2Z 5X3.

FREE GIFT OFFER
084-KEZ

ONE PROOF-OF-PURCHASE

To collect your fabulous FREE GIFT, a cubic zirconia pendant, you must include this original proof-of-purchase for each gift with the properly completed Free Gift Certificate.

084-KEZ

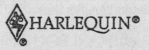

You're About to Become a

Privileged Woman

Reap the rewards of fabulous free gifts and benefits with proofs-of-purchase from Harlequin and Silhouette books

Pages & Privileges™

It's our way of thanking you for buying our books at your favorite retail stores.

PROOF OF PURCHASE
LL-PP23
Offer expires March 31, 1997

**Harlequin and Silhouette—
the most privileged readers in the world!**

For more information about Harlequin and Silhouette's PAGES & PRIVILEGES program call the Pages & Privileges Benefits Desk: 1-503-794-2499

HARLEQUIN ®

LL-PP23